Comfort Creek

YEARLING BOOKS are designed especially to entertain and enlighten young people. Patricia Reilly Giff, consultant to this series, received her bachelor's degree from Marymount College and a master's degree in history from St. John's University. She holds a Professional Diploma in Reading and a Doctorate of Humane Letters from Hofstra University. She was a teacher and reading consultant for many years, and is the author of numerous books for young readers.

Comfort Creek

Joyce McDonald

A YEARLING BOOK

Published by
Bantam Doubleday Dell Books for Young Readers
a division of
Bantam Doubleday Dell Publishing Group, Inc.
1540 Broadway
New York, New York 10036

The trademarks Yearling® and Dell® are registered in the U.S. Patent and Trademark Office and in other countries.

Visit us on the Web! www.bdd.com

Educators and librarians, visit the BDD Teacher's Resource Center at www.bdd.com/teachers

ISBN: 0-440-41198-X

Reprinted by arrangement with Delacorte Press
Printed in the United States of America
February 1998
OPM 10 9 8 7 6 5 4 3 2

For Johanna Schanbacher

And with heartfelt gratitude to my husband, Dwaine,
whose delightful stories of his Florida boyhood
were the inspiration for this book

CONTENTS

Moving

When most folks move, they hire a van and some men to pack up their belongings. Not in Panther Ridge, Florida, though. In Panther Ridge they jack up the house and slide these huge steel beams with wheels on them right under the whole building, attach everything to a big tractor trailer, and drive off.

That's how all us townsfolk moved. One by one, house by house. Some to the Oaks, some to the Pines, and some, like my family, to the middle of nowhere, till nothing was left of Panther Ridge but its name and a forest of stark-naked cinder-block stumps sitting in the dirt.

The day our house was moved, we cruised right down Main Street. Course, we weren't moving much faster than a slug in a snowstorm. My kid sister, Rhonda Fay, and me rode on the front porch, and Pa-Daddy and my big sister, snotty old Louise, rode in the pickup right behind us. Then came my great-grandma Nanny Jo Pearl and her latest husband, E.B. And finally, the rest of the work crew in their trucks. It was a regular little parade.

Louise had slid herself so far down in the front seat of the pickup, all we could see was the top of the dark-green baseball cap her boyfriend, Lloyd, had given her. It looked like Pa-Daddy was escorting a big old watermelon around town. Louise wasn't about to be seen with her family. She thinks she's such a big deal because she's going to be a sophomore in high school next fall.

"Hey, Pa-Daddy," I yelled loud as could be. "Who's the watermelon head you got riding with you?" Louise's head popped up far enough so I could see her eyes, green as Lloyd's baseball cap.

Pa-Daddy pulled his old engineer's cap down over his forehead, stuck his head out the window, and shouted, "Quinnella Jeanne Ellerbee, if you can't behave yourself, you can ride in the back of the truck."

"Me!" I said. "What'd I do? Louise is the one acting like we're all a bunch of Neanderthals she wouldn't be caught dead with."

Pa-Daddy was clenching his teeth. I just smiled back at him, sweet as you please, and started waving to people on the street, which is what folks in a parade are supposed to do. Rhonda Fay sat in the porch rocker, laying low, as they say. Her face was beet red from embarrassment. She and Louise are a lot alike that way.

2

"You think you're some stupid beauty queen riding a parade float," she said. I could hear the rocker squeaking up a storm behind me, but I just kept one hand saddled on the porch rail and the other one busy waving, like I hadn't heard a word. I figured the best thing was to keep myself occupied or I'd have to think about all this moving business. It was downright unnerving. Everything was happening too darn fast. I felt like I'd got myself sucked into a wind tunnel, with no way out.

Just that morning Nanny Jo and me had been packing up the breakables, and the next thing we knew, these men were sliding rails under the house. When we peeked out the back door to see how things were coming along, this red-faced man with a ponytail and the longest mustache I'd ever seen—it curled right under his double chin— climbed into his tractor trailer and backed it up to the beams. I wanted to climb right up on that rig, pound on the window, and tell that red-faced man to put that house right back where it belonged. But, of course, I didn't.

Now all I could do was look down the street at the cinder-block stumps where the houses used to be. Where only the week before I'd been sitting on the front porch, gnawing on sugarcane Nanny Jo had cut from the old Atwell place down the road. I could almost feel those sweet, chewy fibers scrape across my tongue just thinking about it.

There I was, not even a block away and already I was homesick, which might sound pretty strange, considering

3

we were bringing our house with us. But the truth is, a lot of other things go into making a person feel at home. School friends, good neighbors, the Atwells' sugarcane, Mr. Cantrell at the company store tossing in a few extra pieces of red licorice when we bought candy from him.

Besides, just that past May I'd found out I was going to be editor of the sixth-grade newspaper. I'd worked real hard on my grammar all year. Then my fifth-grade teacher, Ms. Prickett, had announced that come fall I'd be the new editor seeing as how, as she said, I've got "a nose for news and a way with words." Only now come fall I wouldn't be editor of anything. We were moving miles from my old school, and Pa-Daddy didn't seem much interested when I pointed out he was ruining my whole life, not to mention any chance I'd ever have of a career in journalism.

Fact is, lately Pa-Daddy doesn't seem interested in anything I do, which is just fine with me, considering we don't see eye to eye on much anymore. Not like the old days when we were buddies. I guess you could say we've been getting on each other's nerves. According to him, he has plenty of problems of his own, which is probably true; he just doesn't mention them as often as I mention mine.

I could feel those first few tears stinging the corners of my eyes. The last thing I needed was for somebody to see me cry. Fortunately I spotted Mrs. Gilchrist sweeping the front porch of the hotel, and I shouted out a big "Hey, how are ya," which got my mind off all that other upsetting stuff. I could hear the rocker scuffing across the floor behind me as Rhonda Fay inched her way up to the railing so she could see what was going on. That's when I spotted Tanner McPherson skateboarding past the hotel.

"Ha!" Rhonda Fay said. "Maybe you want me to think you were waving and grinning at Mrs. Gilchrist, but I know you were really trying to get Tanner McPherson to notice you. You don't fool me for a minute. Or Pa-Daddy, either." It was amazing how Rhonda Fay could manage to sound like Nanny Jo and Pa-Daddy all rolled up into one little nine-year-old tyrant. Anyway, it wasn't true, what she said. I didn't even know Tanner was there when I waved to Mrs. Gilchrist. And I could have cared less whether he noticed me or not.

I looked back at the pickup and saw Pa-Daddy watching me, trying to figure out what I was up to. He doesn't trust Tanner any further than he can throw him.

"What you younguns doing on that porch?" Mrs. Gilchrist narrowed those beady eyes of hers right at us.

"Riding," I said, like Mrs. Gilchrist didn't have a brain in her head, which to my way of thinking is pretty accurate, even if it wasn't polite to say so.

Mrs. Gilchrist was stabbing her porch with the broom. You'd have thought she was churning butter instead of sweeping. "Humph. Getting yourselves killed, is what I think. Pretty foolhardy, if you ask me."

"We didn't ask you," I shouted back, "but thank you anyway, Mrs. Gilchrist."

5

Tanner McPherson got a big laugh out of that. He scraped that skateboard to a screeching halt so he could listen to what else I was gonna tell Mrs. Gilchrist. But I decided to pretend I didn't even notice Tanner standing there. He's had a crush on me ever since first grade when I brought my pet tarantula, Harry, to show-and-tell. The thing is, Rhonda Fay is the one who's sweet on Tanner, even though she's two years younger than we are. Not that I don't think he's cute. It's just that I've been too busy working on my career to bother much with boys lately.

Well, the next thing I knew, old Rhonda Fay had slid off the rocker and was setting her backside on the edge of the porch where the steps used to be. She crossed her legs and started bouncing one leg up and down real casual. Didn't fool me, though. I knew she was showing off her new sneakers for Tanner.

I stared down at my own bare feet. My toes looked like little lead bullets, all grimy and sandy gray, with funny little creases where the dirt had settled in. I hate wearing shoes, any kind of shoes, sneakers included.

Rhonda Fay's sneakers were pure white. Not a smudge of dirt on them. Every summer we each get a new pair of supermarket sneakers. But this year Rhonda Fay raised a real ruckus and absolutely refused to wear sneakers bought at the supermarket.

Pa-Daddy just ignored her. But wouldn't you know she ended up charming Nanny Jo Pearl into taking her all the way to Lakeland to a "*real* shoe store" at a "*real* mall." And don't think we'll ever hear the end of it, either.

I guess Rhonda Fay was hoping she could wrap old Tanner around her little sneaker. But then Mary Alice Taylor came waltzing out the front door of the hotel. Mary Alice is Mrs. Gilchrist's granddaughter. I'm pretty sure she inherited her grandmother's pea brain. Also, Mary Alice is the same age as me and Tanner. She has this glossy, dark hair that hangs clear down to her waist. Mary Alice is darn proud of her hair and never lets anybody forget it. She also happens to have a crush on Tanner. The other thing is, Ms. Prickett went and asked her to be the new editor of the newspaper when she found out I was moving. I just wish she'd picked anybody but snotty old pea-brained Mary Alice.

I was still pretending like I didn't know Tanner existed, but I couldn't help noticing Mary Alice waving to him from the hotel porch, even though he just ignored her.

"Hey, Quinn," Tanner said. Then he added, "Hey, Rhonda Fay," but I could tell he was just being polite. He came right up to the side of our house and started demonstrating some fancy turns and spins on his skateboard.

"Hey, yourself," I said, trying not to look impressed.

That's when the man on the roof, who was up there making sure we didn't run into any wires or cables, yelled at Tanner for riding alongside the house. Told him he had no more sense than a cabbage. Rhonda Fay let out this ridiculous squeaky giggle she's got, which is downright annoying.

Tanner backed off, and the next thing we knew, old Mary Alice had hopped on her bike and was following alongside him down the road.

"Wish this old house would move faster'n five miles an hour," I said.

"Why?" Rhonda Fay asked. "We ain't going nowhere special."

"Aren't. Aren't going anywhere special."

"Well, if it *ain't* the grammar queen."

"Shut up, Rhonda Fay." It was a pretty poor comeback, but I was so mad I couldn't think straight. I hate being made fun of when all I'm trying to do is get my family to talk proper once in a while.

"Anyway, I don't much care about where we're going," I said, "just how fast. I want this house to *fly!*"

Rhonda Fay nodded her agreement and tossed her head like we were already flying and she could feel the wind in her face and through her blond hair. Maybe she was thinking that, if we went fast enough, we could catch up with Mary Alice and Tanner. Or maybe she was thinking about Mary Alice's shiny, long hair.

As for me, I don't get all that concerned about things like hair, my own being pretty pathetic. Kind of no-color hair. I guess the closest it comes to matching anything is the color of a brown-paper sack, which, as far as I'm concerned, is no color at all. It's not very long, either.

Rhonda Fay says it looks like I got an old shaving brush stuck on the back of my head whenever I try to wear it in a ponytail, which is what I was doing that morning on account of it being so hot and all.

"How much further?" I shouted to Pa-Daddy.

"A good ten miles," he shouted back. "We got a long ways to go yet."

The sun was almost overhead by now, and it was getting hotter by the minute. My T-shirt was already soaked with sweat. So far it had been the hottest July on record. I sat down in the rocker, slid it back into the shade, and tried to imagine what life after Panther Ridge would be like. I kept telling myself this moving business didn't much matter, because we had bigger problems to think about. Like the rumors going around that the mining company was running out of money and might have to lay some folks off. Or worse, close down the mine.

I watched Pa-Daddy beating his thumbs on the steering wheel, keeping time to some music on the radio, singing at the top of his lungs. He sure didn't look like a man about to lose his job. Maybe they were just rumors after all.

The Swamp

It took near half the afternoon to get where we were going. For lunch Rhonda Fay and me ate cold chicken and biscuits from the bucket of ice Nanny Jo had packed them in. Meanwhile the house crawled along the highway. A snail pulling a stagecoach could have made better time.

We finally came to some back road. Hardly room for another car to squeeze by. Rhonda Fay got to looking pretty worried all of a sudden, so I stood up to investigate the scenery. Not much to see. A lot of marshy stuff on both sides of the road. Plenty of palmettos and twisted old cypress trees growing in pools of green water. Cypress ponds, we call them. Nothing we hadn't seen before.

Suddenly the house came to a stop by a dirt road. I saw the ponytail man hop out of his rig and meander back to have a word with Pa-Daddy. That's when my stomach decided to do a few flip-flops. Pa-Daddy wasn't bringing us out here to the swamp to live, was he? I mean he wouldn't do that to his own flesh and blood, would he?

Well, I guess something in me snapped right then and there, because the next minute, there I was, fists on hips, screaming loud as you please, "I ain't living in no swamp, you hear? Y'all turn this house around right now!" My grammar always does a bit of backsliding when I'm mad.

Pa-Daddy didn't even look up, just kept talking to the ponytail man. Rhonda Fay was staring at me like my face was about to explode or something.

"Your head's gonna burst, you keep that up," she said. "Blood's gonna spurt right outta your eye sockets."

I could feel my nostrils flaring like a dragon's. Rhonda Fay's eyes got to be the size of quarters. I think she was expecting me to breathe fire over the whole lot of them, which, considering the way I was feeling, would have been fine with me.

"We aren't backwoods." I spit each word at Pa-Daddy like they were hot coals. "We're townsfolk. Next thing you know, all my friends will be calling me the Swamp Thing. I am *not* living in a swamp! You hear?"

Rhonda Fay stabbed a panicky look at her new sneakers. I could tell she was thinking they would never stay white in a place like this. "Me neither," she announced, stamping her foot in protest and raising a little cloud of dust. This was something new, me and Rhonda Fay fighting on the same side for a change.

11

That's when I figured out why Pa-Daddy had never bothered mentioning to us where the land was that Granddaddy Ellerbee had left him. He must have known how we would take it. I guess Louise finally noticed what was going on because she had her head folded into her arms on the dashboard, like she was facing a head-on collision and couldn't bear to look. I think maybe she was even crying.

Up till then Pa-Daddy had been eyeing my antics from a safe distance. Now he and the ponytail man began heading our way.

"You kids sit down now. We're turning in here." Pa-Daddy shifted his weight—which is a lot to shift, take my word for it—and started back toward the pickup.

"This here dirt road?" I rolled my eyes skyward for emphasis. "I mean it, Pa-Daddy, I'm not living anyplace down that dirt road."

"That's just fine, Quinnella honey." Without bothering to turn around, he shouted back over his shoulder, "Why don't you just hop down then and step aside? We got a house to move."

Pa-Daddy was almost to the pickup when I jumped down and ran up to him. "Nobody's asked how me and Rhonda Fay or Louise feel about this moving business. Nobody cares if our whole lives have been ruined." I dug my toes in the sand. "This is where I draw the line," I said, dragging my foot through the soil. And I meant it, too.

12

Pa-Daddy stared down at the line like it was the Grand Canyon itself. We eyeballed each other from opposite sides. I didn't so much as blink. I couldn't afford to lose the first round.

Pa-Daddy turned and hopped up into the pickup, then leaned out the window. "Don't you worry, darlin'," he said, just as cool as you please. He tugged at the brim of his faded old hat. "Bound to be someone along sooner or later to give you a lift to wherever it is you two are planning on going."

I looked back at Rhonda Fay, who had suddenly decided to plunk herself back down on the porch. I guess she needed more time to plan where it was she wanted to go. But I wasn't giving up so easy. "Mom would have hated this," I shouted up at him as I headed back to the house.

I heard Pa-Daddy swallow some air. "We all got to live someplace," he shouted after me, pretending like I'd never even brought up Mom. "Some of us got fewer choices than others. Now why can't you be like Louise, here. She's taking all this like a real trouper." With that, he set the truck engine to roaring and, like it or not, we were on our way again.

Some trouper, I thought. It was pretty obvious, to me anyway, that Louise's face wasn't the color of a plum and wet as an old dishrag from keeping a stiff upper lip.

Course, I knew Pa-Daddy wasn't entirely to blame. Fact is, none of this would have happened if the Panther Ridge Phosphate Mining Company hadn't been in such a bad way. Panther Ridge had always been a company town. And the mining company took care of everything. We had a company store, company hotel, company doctor. Then one day the company announced it couldn't afford us anymore. Said folks could choose to buy the houses they had been renting all their lives. But in the end the company just up and shut down the town anyway.

My family had voted to buy the house, even though it meant borrowing money from the bank, which the Ellerbees had never ever done before. But Pa-Daddy explained we couldn't afford to rent at today's prices, almost double what they had been in the company town. Besides, Pa-Daddy told us the company was selling the houses practically for a song, so they wouldn't have to take care of them anymore. Anyway, like Pa-Daddy said, I guess we didn't have much choice. Not that that made me feel any better.

Rhonda Fay hadn't opened her mouth since we'd turned onto the dirt road. She had this little mustache of sweat on her upper lip, and wormy strands of hair stuck to the sides of her face. She looked plumb wore out. Her T-shirt and cutoffs were so sweaty they looked like she'd put them on right out of the washing machine.

"You shouldn't have said anything about Mom," she scolded.

"Who cares. It's true, isn't it? Mom would have hated this place."

"But she wouldn't have said so." Rhonda Fay pushed a

sweaty clump of bangs away from her forehead. It stood straight up like some old hen's ruffled feathers. But I didn't tell her, even though it was all I could do to keep from laughing out loud.

"No, she'd just move on if she didn't like it," I snapped back. Rhonda Fay looked out over the porch railing like she hadn't even heard me. See, the thing is, Pa-Daddy won't let us talk about Mom. He won't even let us write to her or call her on the phone. Not since she went off nearly two years ago to play with some Kentucky bluegrass band.

On the day she got her first job, we had this big celebration. Pa-Daddy even brought home a store-bought ice-cream cake for the occasion. I guess you could say my mom is pretty talented, even though she never could read a note of music. She plays the guitar and fiddle by ear. She was always listening to this music played by folks I've never even heard of. Folks with names like Flatt and Scruggs, and Jimmy Martin, and Bill Monroe. Sometimes she'd sit by the CD player with her guitar and start playing right along with the album. She called it jamming. And she wasn't half bad, either. Personally, I'd rather listen to Madonna. But I did like this one singer, Alison Krauss. Mom used to play her stuff all the time.

At first Mom played with a local band. Then after about a year, she took up with a new group that traveled out of state a lot. We thought she was just going to be traveling a few months out of the year. But her letters got fewer and fewer, then turned into postcards that said things like "Really miss you kids" and "Sorry I can't make it home for Quinnella's birthday." I think maybe she got used to the traveling life. Maybe it's addictive for some folks.

Then last March we finally got a long letter from her. The longest one she'd ever written. She said she loved us all and stuff, but she'd recently taken up singing and wanted to be free to, as she put it, "explore new career possibilities." Pa-Daddy wouldn't even talk about Mom after that. Still doesn't. Then in May they got divorced. So I guess it was pretty rotten of me bringing her up and all. But Pa-Daddy wasn't the only one angry at Mom. If she was still around, maybe things would have turned out different. The other thing is, I can't even look at a store-bought ice-cream cake anymore without wanting to throw up.

A few minutes later we turned into a big clearing. The men took two sets of what they called temporary stairs and set one by the front porch and one by the back. The problem was, the stairs didn't reach all the way up to the porch, on account of the house was still on the tractor trailer. Then the ponytail man climbed into a pickup with his buddies, and they all headed down the road, leaving the house and trailer sitting right in the middle of the pasture.

Next thing I knew, Nanny Jo Pearl was marching up the front steps with an old dish towel hanging from her pocket. Nanny Jo still has a lot of spunk as far as great-grandmas go, even though she reminds me of a little bird sometimes, kind of small and wiry. And she's got this wispy yellow-white hair that makes me think of feathers. Nobody really knows how old she is. She's never told anybody. But Louise and me once figured out she was at least eighty-five.

"Well, come on, get up," she said, pulling me by the arm and tapping Rhonda Fay with the toe of her slipper. Nanny Jo wears bedroom slippers all the time because she's got bunions. "We got us a house to set up."

I yanked my arm from her tight grip. "Nanny Jo," I said, "the house is still on the truck."

"We got a dinner to cook, Quinny girl," Nanny Jo said. "Don't matter if we eat it on a truck or on the ground." She stood there on the porch with her knotty old fists punched into her waist and her lips squooshed together like she'd been sucking on a lemon. "Humph," she said, looking around. "It ain't exactly Comfort Creek, but I guess with a little tending, it'll do." She pointed to the railing. "Get yourself some flower boxes. That'll help some."

Comfort Creek isn't a real place. It's just this town Nanny Jo made up. When we were little, she used to tell us stories about the folks who lived there, like they were real people. And sometimes, when I listened to her, it seemed like they *were* real. Anyway, now that I'm grown up, I know better. I even looked it up on the map once, so I know for a fact there's no such place. Besides, as far as any of us knows, Nanny Jo has never so much as set her

17

big toe outside the county for as long as she's been on this earth. So she couldn't have been anyplace like that. But she still swears Comfort Creek really exists. She's just never bothered to tell us where, which is why I'm pretty sure she made it all up.

That night we had to cook on Pa-Daddy's Coleman stove—the one he uses for camping out—because we didn't have any propane gas for our regular stove. But Pa-Daddy said we would get that all situated soon enough. We also had to cook with store-bought water because the plumbing wasn't hooked up.

Thank goodness Nanny Jo hung around long enough to cook the black-eyed peas and tomato gravy before she and E.B. headed back home. Louise can't cook worth a darn. She lumps the tomato gravy every time. Makes great crackling corn bread, though. But that's about the only thing she knows how to make.

We didn't have any electricity either, so Nanny Jo filled all the kerosene lanterns before she left. They stood ready and waiting on the kitchen counter. Five of them. All in a neat line like little metal soldiers. It would be dark in an hour, and they would be all the light we'd have.

Pa-Daddy was busy cutting up an onion to sprinkle on top of his dinner. I hadn't said one single word to him since we'd gotten there, but I was desperate to find out what was going to happen next. I didn't want any more unpleasant surprises. So I decided on a temporary truce.

I leaned across the table and grabbed a chunk of the corn bread we'd brought with us. "Nanny Jo says the men are coming back tomorrow to put up cinder blocks."

"That's about right." Pa-Daddy went right on cutting up his onion.

"They're gonna lower the house on the cinder blocks and take the tractor trailer away?"

"I reckon that's what they'll do."

"Are they going to hook up the plumbing?"

"Not much point."

"Why? We got a well, right? Nanny Jo said so. And we got a septic tank."

"No electricity." Pa-Daddy bit off a chunk of corn bread. Two of his teeth on the left side were missing. I stared into that black hole in his mouth while I tried to get my bearings.

"Don't need electricity for water," I said, like I knew what I was talking about.

"Sure you do. Can't get running water without a pump. Can't run the pump without electricity. Course, I'll try to get somebody to hook up a manual pump in the meantime."

"What else isn't going to run?" Louise said as she set a bowl of greens on the table. I could see she was starting to get nervous. Rhonda Fay set her fork down, like she

19

couldn't swallow another bite until she'd had her nightly dose of bad news.

Pa-Daddy looked kind of thoughtful for a minute, then up and said, pleasant as you please, "Well, the toilet, I guess."

"What?" The three of us gasped.

"Can't flush it," he said, real matter-of-fact.

"What are we gonna do?" Louise moaned.

"Well, I've already thought about that." He stood up real deliberate and waved us to the back door. "See there," he said, pointing down the slope a ways to some little building below. "You can use that for now."

"Is that what I think it is?" Rhonda Fay asked, grabbing hold of my wrist like this was all my doing.

"It's an outhouse," Pa-Daddy said, I guess to make sure we all understood.

Well, Nanny Jo was right about one thing: this place sure wasn't Comfort Creek. In fact, this whole moving business was turning out to be a real nightmare. And on top of everything else, we didn't even have a bathroom. What could Pa-Daddy have been thinking? Bringing three girls to a place with no bathroom was like skydiving without a parachute—downright life-threatening. No doubt about it, Pa-Daddy had really gone and done it this time. As far as I was concerned, me and him were officially at war.

Bugs

"Somebody better find me a big old jelly jar because I'm not peeing in no hole in the ground." Louise slammed her hands on her hips and squinted her eyes into the dark.

Me and Louise were on the front porch waiting for Rhonda Fay to come back from the outhouse with the flashlight. There wasn't any moon. Not even a star in the sky. The night was as black as tar. Suddenly the outhouse door flew open and a ball of light came streaking up the hill toward the house. It was Rhonda Fay, and she was about fit to be tied. "There's spiders in there," she said, practically flinging the flashlight at Louise. "How's a person to concentrate with all those things crawling around?"

"You got toilet paper stuck to the bottom of your sneaker there, Rhonda Fay," I said, pointing to the white streamer trailing behind her.

"Ugh. This place is disgusting." She scraped the toilet paper off on the step. "I'm calling Nanny Jo and seeing if I can move in with her."

"How you going to call her when we don't even have a phone?" Louise said, slapping that old flashlight against the palm of her hand like she couldn't quite decide whether to use it to find the outhouse or hit somebody with it.

Rhonda Fay flopped onto the porch, bent over, and put her head in her lap. Her skinny legs dangled over the edge. The toes of her sneakers barely reached the top step. "I hate this place," she said, sobbing into her lap.

"Hush up," Louise hissed. "You want Pa-Daddy to hear you?"

"Yes." She looked up at Louise with such a pitiful face, I almost felt bad for her. Almost. But I was still pretty busy feeling sorry for myself. "Maybe he'll change his mind if he knows this place is making us all miserable," she said.

"I'd just as soon hop the next bus out of here, myself," Louise said, keeping her voice low. "Course, I haven't got the faintest idea where the nearest bus stop is. My guess would be about a hundred miles away, from the looks of things."

Like Rhonda Fay and Louise, I didn't much want to be where we were. But something didn't feel right. It was like we were plotting a mutiny behind Pa-Daddy's back. Not that he didn't deserve it. But I'd spent so many years sticking up for my dad that I had to admit, these bad feelings just didn't set well. Then I remembered how he had

22

brought us to this place without even asking how we felt about it, and I started to get mad all over again. I could feel the blood burning the tips of my ears. He was going to pay for this.

"Rhonda Fay," Louise said, sitting down next to her and using her most adult voice, "I don't think we got a whole lotta choice. Pa-Daddy couldn't afford to buy a house *and* land." I tried to see Pa-Daddy's side of the situation, too, like Louise was doing, but it just wasn't working. "This is the only land the Ellerbees own outright," she said, "except for Nanny Jo's place. You want to make Pa-Daddy feel bad?"

Sometimes Louise drove me crazy switching sides like that midbattle. The fact is, I needed her to be angry with Pa-Daddy right then. I needed all of us to stick together.

"Well, leave it to the Ellerbees to buy land in the middle of some swamp." Rhonda Fay let out a disgusted sigh, lowered her head back into her lap, and circled it with her arms.

Thank goodness Rhonda Fay wasn't deserting me. "Nanny Jo always said the Ellerbee men had no head for business," I volunteered.

Louise stood up and sized me up for another minute, like she couldn't decide whether or not to argue this point, then handed me the flashlight. "I got to find me a jelly jar someplace," she said, letting the front door bang behind her.

One thing we found out that first night was that the mosquitoes in the swamp were a lot worse than they were back in Panther Ridge, which was about the worst anybody could imagine. Louise was trying to read her movie magazine by the light of the kerosene lamp in our bedroom, but I figured she must have been having a pretty hard time concentrating, with all the slapping noises we were making.

We had plastered Band-Aids over the bigger holes in the window screen, but they weren't helping much. Rhonda Fay was about driving me crazy flip-flopping back and forth in our bed, flailing her arms every which way. Me and Rhonda Fay had to share the double bed. Naturally, Louise got the single bed, her being the oldest and all. That's about all the furniture our little bedroom could hold, except for a small dresser—we each got one drawer all to ourselves—and a nightstand.

I lay there trying not to think about the mosquitoes, but every time I opened my eyes and looked at the ceiling, my skin started to crawl. There had to be hundreds of them flying around up there. And when they buzzed around my ear it about drove me stark raving mad.

Next thing I knew, I'd grabbed a newspaper that was lying between the beds, got a good bouncing motion going on the bed, and began swatting the heck out of those critters.

Louise looked up from her magazine. "Well, if this isn't a pretty sight. Mosquito guts all over the ceiling."

"That's *our* blood up there on that ceiling, not theirs," I told her, without missing a bounce. "This is war."

"What you swatting them with?" Louise stood up in her bed to get a better look. "Hey, give me that. That's my latest *National Enquirer*. I haven't even seen it yet."

She ripped the paper out of my hand. "Oh fine. Will you look at this?" She stuck the paper right smack in front of my face.

" 'Senator and Wife Adopt Space Alien's Baby,' " I read out loud.

"I mean the blood, you idiot. How can a person read this with half the words covered in mosquito blood?"

"Our blood," I reminded her.

"Do . . . you . . . *mind!*" Rhonda Fay said. "I've had a very bad day, and I would like to get some sleep." She rolled over and pulled the sheet up over her head, I expect to keep out the mosquitoes, although it had to be a hundred degrees under there. "Between folks slamming mosquitoes and grinding their teeth in their sleep, it's a wonder a person gets any rest at all around here," she mumbled from under her sheet tent.

Rhonda Fay and Louise have been tormenting me because I've been grinding my teeth at night. Louise says if I keep it up much longer I'll have nothing left but little white stumps in my mouth. Nanny Jo says folks grind their teeth in their sleep because they're mad as blazes about something. Well, if that's true, I hope I get over being mad before I have to gum my food like Nanny Jo does when she doesn't have her false teeth in.

I crawled back under the sheet and stared up at the ceiling. Mosquito parts squashed all over the ceiling may not have been a pretty sight, but it was a lot better than listening to all those live ones buzzing in my ear. Unfortunately I'd hardly made a dent.

Louise punched her pillow a few times, then settled down to finish her magazine. "Three more years," she grumbled. "Three more years and I'll be out of here."

This is Louise's favorite chant. It changes every year. Last year, all we ever heard was "Four more years, just four more years." I swear she even marks off the days on some secret calendar.

Louise has got it all figured out. She says as soon as she's eighteen she's heading for Hollywood. She's aspiring to be a game-show hostess. That's all she's talked about since she was ten. She says she can't think of a better job. You get to wear a new dress every night and show off the great prizes that folks have won. You get to look pretty and make folks happy all at the same time. She takes it very serious. Never misses a single game show on TV. Makes notes on what the hostesses wear, how they do up their hair, how they move. I guess you might say it's sort of a calling. So naturally Louise is pretty upset about us not having electricity, which means she can't watch her game shows.

Sometimes, when I can't sleep, I get Louise to tell me

the story of how Vanna White got to be on *Wheel of Fortune*. This is just about Louise's favorite story. And it really helps me fall asleep.

I got to admit, Louise is pretty enough to be a game-show hostess. She has this real soft light-brown hair that gets kind of gold streaks across the top of it from the sun, like Mom's. It's naturally curly, too. Me and Rhonda Fay didn't get one measly ounce of curl in our hair. We figure it must have got all used up on Louise. Anyway, me and Rhonda Fay work real hard to make sure Louise's looks don't go to her head, but so far it hasn't worked.

I got to wondering if living in a swamp was going to interfere with Louise's career plans like it was with mine. What could possibly happen out here in the middle of nowhere? Not having anything to write about could really squash a reporter's instincts. I mean, did Diane Sawyer grow up in some swamp? Did Connie Chung? They made a point of being where the big stories were breaking. That's how they got to be famous.

If I was ever going to make it as a journalist, I'd have to figure a way out of here. Right then I made up my mind that living in this old swamp wasn't going to stop me from getting where I wanted to go. Not even Pa-Daddy could stop me, even though he'd already messed things up for me pretty bad.

The Bad-News Blues

By the end of the first week, we were getting used to hauling water from the stream so we could wash our hair and clothes. The ponytail man had come back and lowered our house onto the cinder blocks and attached the stairs, so we didn't have to risk breaking our necks jumping from the porch to the top step anymore. The worst part was not having a TV. Louise had this radio that ran on batteries, but she kept hogging it. Took it everywhere she went. When Louise left the house with that radio, it was like the whole outside world went with her.

We were all pretty desperate for just about any entertainment. We'd only been there a week, but things were so bad I'd actually taken to reading Louise's movie magazines. I'd even thought about asking Pa-Daddy to drive me over to the Pines to see some of my friends, even though it was a good ten miles away. But I was still on a talking strike. I hadn't said two words to Pa-Daddy since the night we found out we didn't have plumbing—not that he noticed, or anything.

Then we got more bad news. We were right in the middle of dinner when Pa-Daddy announced real casual that it was going to cost thousands of dollars for the electric company to run lines from the main road to our house. But it didn't come as any surprise to me. I'd been expecting something like this, considering how he'd been so sneaky about everything else. I just wished he'd saved the news till we were done eating.

"So borrow the money," Louise said, like we got a tree full of hundred-dollar bills outside, just ripe for picking.

Pa-Daddy gave her one of his sorrowful looks. "Already borrowed to buy the house, darlin', and to have the well and septic dug. Banks ain't bottomless pits. They don't keep handing out money just because somebody needs it. Fact is, I couldn't get them to go any higher on the mortgage."

"This is pretty poor planning, Pa-Daddy," Rhonda Fay chimed in.

"It ain't like we won't have electricity eventually," he said. "We're gonna have to save up for it, that's all."

I couldn't even look at Pa-Daddy right then, I was so embarrassed for him. I slid my chair away from the table and began clearing dishes without anyone even asking me to help.

"Well, we at least got us a stove and oven," he said, trying to make things sound better than they were. "Now that them propane bottles have been hooked up, you don't have to use the camping stove no more."

Louise and Rhonda Fay didn't bother to look up from the table; they just kept pushing the food on their plates from one side to the other, like they hadn't even heard him.

"Tell you what I'm gonna do," he said, sounding like some used-car salesman about to give us a great bargain. "I'm gonna fix us up a hand pump so we'll have running water in the kitchen."

I could feel Pa-Daddy talking right to my back, but I didn't turn around. I poured some water from a jug into the dishpan and started washing cups. I knew Pa-Daddy wanted things to be different, but I told myself I didn't care.

Nobody was saying anything about the hand-pump idea, so I snuck a peek over my shoulder. Pa-Daddy looked real disappointed. "Hey. Tomorrow's Saturday," he said, trying to look cheerful. "What do you say we all take a day and head up to E.B.'s camp, maybe catch us a mess of mullet?"

E.B. owns this fish camp on the Gulf Coast. He used to run it seven days a week before he married Nanny Jo.

Then he started managing Nanny Jo's orange groves and only going up to the camp on Saturdays. E.B.'s nephew, Tyler, takes care of the camp the rest of the time.

A fish camp is a place where folks rent space to pitch their tents or park their trailers so they can spend a lot of time fishing. Sometimes they even rent cabins.

"Go fishing?" Louise's upper lip curled so high it almost touched the tip of her nose. "No thanks."

"No thanks," added Rhonda Fay, sounding just like Louise.

Pa-Daddy looked downright dejected. Then he did an about-face and started barking orders again. "Well, I'm going, and I'm not leaving three kids here alone. So you'd better plan on it."

Seemed like every day we were having less and less say about things around here. Louise and Rhonda Fay just sat there. But something got a grip on me right then. My whole body was shaking like some inside earthquake was working its way out. I snapped up Pa-Daddy's favorite Elvis coffee mug from the dishpan and hurled it to the floor with all my might. I wanted it to shatter into a million pieces, but the mug was so thick it landed with a thunk. Only the handle broke off. I stared down at the soapy mess on the floor, afraid to look over at Pa-Daddy. I heard his chair sliding away from the table, and those heavy footsteps of his crossing the room. I kept my eyes on the mug like I could will it back into one piece again.

Then I saw his hand lift the broken handle. "Better be more careful, Quinn," he said, his voice soft and low. "Let's see if we can't glue this back together."

———

The next morning, while it was still dark, we headed out for the Gulf Coast. Louise rode with Pa-Daddy in the front of the pickup, and me and Rhonda Fay stretched out in the back, letting the wind make a tangled mess of our hair. It takes about two hours to get to E.B.'s fish camp, but it's worth it (although I wasn't about to admit it that morning). Nanny Jo always takes part of our catch and fries them up for our lunch. There isn't anything better than golden fried mullet. Sweet as butter on your tongue.

Soon as E.B. saw us, he came right over and swooped us out of the back of the truck. He's still pretty strong even though he must be at least eighty. I figure it's because he still tends Nanny Jo's orange groves, which probably gives him plenty of exercise. But that doesn't help his eyesight any. Truth is, E.B.'s glasses are so thick they make his eyes look twice their size. He always looks like he's surprised to see us, even when he isn't.

None of us knew what the E.B. actually stood for, seeing as how Nanny Jo has always called her husbands by their initials. Seemed like by the time we finally found out their full names, they were always gone—one way or the other. She had already outlived three husbands and divorced two more. I guess you could say getting married is just about Nanny Jo's favorite pastime.

E.B. seemed pretty pleased to see us, even though he hadn't been expecting company. But he couldn't fish with us right then because he had to make his rounds of the camp. He likes to make sure the folks renting his cabins are doing okay.

The sun was just peeking over the treetops by the inlet when Pa-Daddy cast the net from the dock. The neat thing about the dock is that it isn't permanently attached, so it moves up and down with the tide. The tide was low, and we could see a whole mess of mullet right below. Got to fish when the tide's low, otherwise by the time the net gets down to the bottom, those fish have beat fins for safer territory.

First throw Pa-Daddy didn't catch anything. Second time he pulled up five, and Louise put them right in the croaker sack. That's what Nanny Jo's second husband, C.Q., used to call it. I don't know why, because it's only an old burlap bag. Mom once told me folks called it a croaker sack because that's where the fish croak, so to speak, which is pretty disgusting if it's true. But I think she was just kidding. Anyway, Louise put the mullet in the sack, tied it, and lowered it back into the water. Every now and then the dock rolled under our feet, reminding us the tide was coming in, slow but sure.

Thinking about Mom made me feel like some big old

sigh had swallowed up my insides. It was the first time we'd been to the fish camp since Mom and Dad got divorced. Mom always used to come fishing with us, even though she about drove Pa-Daddy crazy feeding Fritos and potato chips to the fish. He must have told her a hundred times that the whole idea was the fish were supposed to fill *our* bellies, not the other way around. But Mom never minded what he said. She would keep right on tossing junk food in the inlet and watching the fish bubble to the surface. They came so close, she could have picked them right up in her hand. But she never did.

I wondered if Pa-Daddy was thinking about Mom. I wondered if he was wishing we hadn't come to the camp. But if it bothered him, he didn't show it. He just kept working that net, pulling in the mullet.

By midmorning the tide was getting too high to fish, so we headed on over to E.B.'s bait shop and lunch counter to see if Nanny Jo would fry us up a plateful of mullet. At first we thought no one was there, and I could tell Pa-Daddy was real disappointed. But then here came Nanny Jo from around back, pulling this little rusty wagon full of potted flowers.

She didn't look at all surprised to see us. Just nodded a silent howdy, like she'd been waiting for us to show up. But there wasn't any way she could have known we were coming. And E.B. was off on his rounds, so he couldn't have told her. That's just how Nanny Jo is. She's got this second sight, which means she senses things real good. She thinks maybe I got second sight, too, but it's too early to tell.

Nanny Jo pointed to the plants and then to the flower boxes under the store windows. "Thought I'd try the real thing."

Long as I'd been coming to E.B.'s fish camp, there'd never been anything but plastic geraniums in those boxes.

"Fine idea." Pa-Daddy nodded his approval.

Nanny Jo lifted her brown, liver-spotted hand and waved a wrinkled finger at the croaker sack. "Good catch?"

"Got us about four dozen," Pa-Daddy said.

"Well, bring 'em on in." She parked her wagon under the window. "We'll fry us up a mess. I'll put the rest on ice for you. E.B. should be back anytime now. Fact, soon as he smells that mullet frying, he'll be here quicker'n you can sneeze."

Louise and Rhonda Fay were helping themselves to a couple of RCs from the soda machine. Pa-Daddy had already parked himself on the top step of the porch and was staring out over the inlet. So I followed Nanny Jo inside. Within no time at all, she had those mullet snapping and crackling in the hot lard. I pulled up a stool and watched Nanny Jo roll the next batch of fish in the flour. When my mom lived with us, she always used to help with the flouring while Nanny Jo did the frying.

"Thinking about your ma, ain't you?" Nanny Jo said, tilting her pointy chin in my direction.

Sometimes that second sight thing could really catch a person off guard. It was all I could do to give her a nod.

"Well, it don't surprise me none. I can't stand here frying mullet without thinking about her working by my side." Nanny Jo brushed the flour from her hands, snapped up a spatula, and flipped over the fish in her big cast-iron skillet.

"Pa-Daddy won't let us talk about her," I blurted out.

Nanny Jo nodded, like that didn't surprise her one little bit. "Did the same thing when his ma died, back when he was twelve."

The thing is, Nanny Jo's more like Pa-Daddy's *mom* than his grandma. She raised him and his brother and sister, Jeb and Phoebe, after their dad, my granddaddy El-lerbee, got himself killed in the Vietnam War. Their mom, my grandma Louise, went and died a few months later because, as Nanny Jo tells it, she didn't have the heart to go on living.

Nanny Jo rinsed off a few more mullet and tossed them into the flour. "Couldn't get him to even mention his ma," she said. "It was like she'd never existed. That boy just don't deal well with losing folks."

"We get in big trouble if we talk about Mom," I said.

"Miss her, do you?"

I nodded.

"Well, she isn't a bad person, Quinn. Lots of spirit. Did

I ever tell you about the time she come to pick up your daddy in her family's tow truck?"

I pretended like I'd never heard this story before, but the truth is I'd been hearing it most of my life, not just from Nanny Jo, but from Mom and Pa-Daddy, and about anybody else in the family who gets in a storytelling mood. And they all tell it different. Still, I wanted to hear it again. About the time Pa-Daddy's truck was in the shop. So Mom—she was Bonnie Hewett back then—came to pick him up at his house instead. And at seven o'clock sharp she came tearing up the driveway in her daddy's tow truck. It was their second date and Pa-Daddy was really looking forward to it. Had big plans to take her to a show over in Lakeland. But they never made it to the movies that night, because they no sooner hit the highway than they came across this friend of my dad's named Joe Whiggs. The transmission in his car had up and died, and there he was stranded by the side of the road. So Mom just pulled over, hooked him up to the tow, and drove him right to her daddy's garage. Pa-Daddy was still hoping they could make the second show, but wouldn't you know they came across someone else broke down on the side of the road, and Mom towed him in, too.

By then Pa-Daddy wasn't too happy, on account of it was Saturday night and they were supposed to be on a date. I mean, there was my dad all dressed up in his brand-new jeans, crisp as a new twenty-dollar bill, smelling like Old Spice, and probably hoping for a good-night kiss. And there was my mom, her hair flying every which way, her face all shiny with sweat, and grease smudges all over her arms, having the time of her life.

Well, Pa-Daddy didn't mind telling her just what he thought about that. But my mom just looked at him, grinning like she'd struck gold, and said, "Why, Claude honey"—that's my daddy's name, Claude William Ellerbee—"I'm getting fifty dollars for towing these folks. You wouldn't want me passing up good money when it just dropped in my lap like that, would you? We can go to that old movie anytime."

Me and Nanny Jo laughed all over again thinking about that. My mom has always been pretty practical when it comes to money. She told Pa-Daddy she didn't get to drive the tow truck much because of her three older brothers. And that night was the first time she'd ever towed anybody's car, which she thought was pretty darn exciting. The thing was, to my mom's way of thinking, that was about the best date she'd ever had. She told my daddy she'd had more fun than if they'd gone to an amusement park.

"Your mama is about the most unpredictable person I know," Nanny Jo said. "Reminds me a lot of Ronnie Whittle, this girl I knew in Comfort Creek. Now *there* was a wild one."

People were always reminding Nanny Jo of folks from Comfort Creek. That's how she usually launched into one of her stories. The best stories, at least to my way of thinking, were always about this kid named Nell, who was about my age and who was always getting herself into trouble.

"You never knew what your mama was going to do next," Nanny Jo was saying. "That's why I like her. Just don't much like what she done to her family." Nanny Jo wiped her hands on a dish towel hanging from her apron pocket and gave me a thoughtful look. "Tell you what. You and me, we'll talk about her as much as you please when we're alone. How's that?"

That was fine with me. And the truth is, I didn't feel a bit guilty breaking Pa-Daddy's rule, seeing as how it wasn't very fair to begin with. I pulled my stool up to the counter. "I can do the flouring part, like Mom did," I said, picking up a fish. "You do the frying part." Nanny Jo gave me one of her we're-in-this-together winks, and I could tell the arrangement was just fine with her.

After a while it started getting pretty hot back there in the kitchen, so I decided to step outside for a little fresh air. Pa-Daddy was still sitting on the step not doing much of anything. I sat myself in the rocking chair and watched the boats. Every time a motorboat went by, the dock bounced around like it was caught in a storm. I thought about going back out on the dock till the fish were ready, maybe riding those motorboat waves for a while, it being somewhat uncomfortable sitting there with me and Pa-Daddy not talking. But then, out of the blue he said, "You kids are growing up so fast," and he shook his head like he didn't know what to do about it.

Inside, Nanny Jo put on the jukebox. Louise and Rhonda Fay wandered back from the soda machine where they'd been hanging out. They plunked their backsides on the front stoop, and the four of us sat there listening to some country-western singer belting out a song called "The Bad-News Blues":

> *Oh, it's been a hard life, darlin'*
> *and it ain't over yet. . . .*

I kept waiting to see what Pa-Daddy was going to say next. That's when he got to laughing so hard, tears spurted outta his eyes. "Now that about says it all, don't it?" he said.

"It isn't that funny, Pa-Daddy," Rhonda Fay said. "It's supposed to be sad."

But he kept shaking his head and wiping back the tears, his big chest heaving with every chuckle. He looked each one of us straight in the eye. "I got a little bad news myself," he said when he finally got himself under control, "and I don't know any way to tell you but straight out. I wanted to tell you last night, but y'all took the news about the electricity so hard. . . ." His voice sputtered to a stop like a car that had run out of gas.

My belly tied itself up so tight it liked to pop open. I was so scared I couldn't say anything—not that I'd been doing all that much talking recently. I just waited.

"It's my job," Pa-Daddy said. "I been laid off."

I was trying to act like I couldn't have cared less, but my heart was thumping and pounding up a storm. It looked like those rumors we'd been hearing were true after all.

"You mean *fired*?" Louise shrieked. "When?"

"Not fired, darlin'. Laid off. It ain't the same thing." Pa-Daddy took a gulp of air and swallowed. "They told us yesterday afternoon. Course, it might only be a temporary layoff. They ain't telling us much right now."

My dad has worked at the phosphate mines almost from the day he decided he didn't need any more education and quit high school a year before he was supposed to graduate. I couldn't imagine him working anywhere else.

"But Pa-Daddy," Louise said, her face all twisted up to hold back the tears, "I thought the company was going to be okay after they didn't have to worry about the town no more."

He shook his head like he still couldn't quite believe it. A clump of dark-red hair flopped across his forehead. "We all thought that. Even after they filed for bankruptcy, we thought they'd surely figure something out. But it ain't gonna happen."

Rhonda Fay sprang to her feet and stood—legs apart, hands on hips—like she was about to give a speech. "We aren't going to live in one of those cardboard boxes on the street like homeless folks, are we?"

"Course not," Pa-Daddy said, trying to reassure her. "We got a roof over our heads, ain't we? We're going to be just fine."

I didn't think it was a good time to remind him that it was the bank that owned the roof over our heads. I figured he'd probably forgot, never having owed anybody anything before.

That's when Rhonda Fay announced she was putting herself up for adoption, to any family with a working bathroom. Louise just kept muttering "Three more years" under her breath.

I decided if I wanted answers I was going to have to break down and talk to Pa-Daddy. But I made up my mind it was only one of those temporary truces. "What are we gonna do?" I asked, trying not to sound panicky.

"Don't know yet."

"You could get another job," I said, in my most practical voice.

Pa-Daddy turned away and stared out over the inlet, like maybe all the answers were someplace over on the other side. "Ain't a real big demand for pit bosses. But I ain't going to worry about it too much, yet. There's still a chance it's only temporary."

Pa-Daddy used to work these high-pressure water guns that wash down the phosphate and make it all muddy so it can be pumped back to the plant. Then he started supervising the men with the water guns instead. Being a pit boss might sound pretty important, but the truth is, it doesn't take a whole lot of know-how. "What about the other mines?" I asked him.

"Cutting back. They're all cutting back. Nobody's hiring right now."

"But it could change, like you said."

"It could." A tiny smile crept into the corner of his mouth. "There is this one thing. There's been talk about a new mining company coming into the Pines. Some big northeastern corporation owns it. They got one located up north of the state, too. Seems they're looking to expand. Last I heard, their geologists announced the Pines is sitting on a mound of phosphate just waiting for the taking."

By now my skin was soaking wet and prickling all over. Maybe Pa-Daddy thought that was good news, but I couldn't help wondering what would happen to all our friends who'd only just moved to the Pines from Panther Ridge. And what about Nanny Jo and E.B.? They lived right on the edge of the Pines. Here was a whole new mess of worries sneaking up on the horizon.

"We ain't going to starve," Pa-Daddy said, trying to keep things calm. "I guess I can go on unemployment for a few months." I could tell that didn't set well with him. Pa-Daddy hates taking anything from anybody, even if it is owed to him.

My heart was beating faster than ever. "Is that gonna be enough?"

He took a big gulp of air. "No, Quinn, it ain't." He started counting stuff off on his fingers like he was trying to keep track of it all, stuff like mortgage payments, and taxes, and insurance. He just kept on and on until I thought my head would burst. Then he looked at us kind of sheepish. "What we definitely ain't going to have for a while is electricity."

We all nodded in unison. We'd pretty much figured that out.

Pa-Daddy circled his fist around his chin and tugged at it for a few minutes, looking thoughtful. Then he lowered his eyes like he'd suddenly spotted something on his boot. "Sure would appreciate it if you girls didn't mention this to anyone right now. Especially Nanny Jo."

"Why not?" Louise asked. "Maybe Nanny Jo would want to help."

"Don't want to worry her," Pa-Daddy said, not looking up from his boots.

I got a funny feeling there was more to it than that. Maybe he already knew the new mining-company business wouldn't set too well with Nanny Jo.

Then he slapped his knee, I guess to let us know we were done talking. "Come on. No point spoiling our day worrying," he said. "Your old pa will figure something out. Let's dig into them mullet."

Louise and Rhonda Fay followed him inside, but I didn't feel much like eating. Even that mouthwatering mullet would have tasted like sand on my tongue right then. Seemed like Pa-Daddy was always serving us bad news with our meals these days. Like maybe he thought the food would make it go down a little easier.

The thing was, I knew I should have felt bad for Pa-Daddy. I should have tried to make it easier for him. He had tried to make it easier on *us,* making it a kind of festive day. But all I could think was that he'd brought us here to soften the blow from another wallop of bad news. E.B.'s is one of my most favorite places on earth, and now I'd never be able to go there again without remembering the day my family finally hit rock bottom. Pa-Daddy had gone and ruined this place for me. And I would never forgive him for that.

5

Cypress Knees

Nanny Jo always says bad things happen in threes. So I guess I should have seen it coming. I mean, first off, the company tells us we got to move. Next thing we know, we're living in some swamp without plumbing or electricity. And then, bingo! the company goes and lays off Pa-Daddy. The only good thing I could think of, while we were riding home from E.B.'s fish camp, was maybe no more bad stuff would happen for a while, us having filled our quota, so to speak.

Well, another week dragged by, and there I was frying up a mess of bacon for breakfast when Louise waltzed into the kitchen and announced she wanted to change her name to Lana.

"What's wrong with the name Louise?" I asked, forking a couple strips of bacon onto a platter. "It was

Grandma Ellerbee's name." Even though Grandma Ellerbee died before any of us were born, Pa-Daddy is always telling us what a fine woman she was, and we more or less take his word for it.

"Grandma Ellerbee wasn't aspiring to be a game-show hostess." Louise yanked a chair away from the kitchen table and parked herself sideways, like she wasn't sure whether she'd be staying for breakfast or not. "A game-show hostess has to have a glamorous name. Louise is such a . . ." I could see she was groping around for the right word. ". . . such a sensible name."

I figured Louise probably picked the name Lana because it sounded a little like Vanna. Course, Louise looked like anyone but Vanna White—especially that morning with her hair all stringy and matted to her head, seeing as how we don't have a shower. If anybody wants to take a bath around here they have to get themselves a bar of soap and a towel and head down to the creek.

"Well, you're right about that," I said. "You're not exactly the sensible type."

Louise got this snotty look on her face, like she always does when she's getting ready to put you in your place. "I wouldn't talk if I was you. Being named after some old horse-race bet ain't exactly something I'd care to brag about."

I would have told Louise to shut her stupid mouth, but that's pretty hard to do when you know somebody's telling the truth. And she was right, Mom did name me after a dumb old bet, except she added an extra *n* to my name so it wouldn't be so obvious to folks.

I have Nanny Jo's fifth husband, S.T., to thank for that. He's the one who took Mom to her first horse race back before I was born. Nanny Jo about had a fit when she heard. To her way of thinking, gambling is right up there at the top of the list when it comes to being sinful, which is why she finally ended up divorcing old S.T. He kept gambling away all the profits from the orange groves.

But on the day S.T. took my mom to the races, wouldn't you know she'd win two hundred dollars on a quinella. That's where you have to pick not just the first-place horse, but also the second-place one in order to win anything. Anyway, my mom decided right then and there that *quinella* was about the prettiest word she'd ever heard, and she decided right then and there that's what she was going to name her next born. Naturally, the next born turned out to be me. Mom always told me that *quinella* meant "lucky." Well, maybe for her it was. But I don't much consider it all that lucky for me.

"I like the name Louise better than Lana," Rhonda Fay said, biting down on a piece of bacon with her pointy teeth. Rhonda Fay's got these sharp little teeth on either side of her mouth. Not as long as a vampire's, but they're getting there.

I wondered if maybe Louise thought by changing her name she could change who she was . . . maybe even where she was from. Maybe she thought by changing her name, she'd suddenly find herself living someplace with plumbing.

I plunked down a plate of grits in front of her. I wanted to tell her I didn't think it was that easy, but instead all I said was, "Well you named Pa-Daddy and he named you, so it's a fair trade." This is true. When Louise was learning to talk, she couldn't make up her mind what to call Pa-Daddy. So she just slapped her two choices together.

Louise took a fork and mashed her grits flat as a pancake. "That's no reason not to change it if I want."

"Okay by me." I slid some sunny-side-ups on top of her grits. "Except I think you need a parent's permission if you're not eighteen."

I could hear Louise grumbling "Three more years" under her breath while she mushed the egg yolks into her grits and topped them off with a dash of salt and pepper. "Don't think I won't," she said. "In the meantime, y'all can start calling me plain Lana."

Rhonda Fay and me exchanged looks. Cows would fly to the moon before I ever called her Lana.

"Okay, Plain Lana," Rhonda Fay said. "That's about the fittingest name you come up with yet."

Louise puffed up like some angry old pigeon and was about to explode into a mess of nasty words when Pa-Daddy came through the door with two folks we'd never seen before.

"Found these folks on my walk," he announced. "Seems they're our neighbors."

"We got neighbors?" Rhonda Fay looked real surprised. I guess she figured nobody else would actually choose to live out here.

Pa-Daddy tipped his hand toward the two strangers. "This here's Steve Murdoch and his son, Ed Earl."

Steve Murdoch swept off his cap and stuffed it in his back pocket, real gentlemanly, and gave us a nod. Right off he reminded me of the scarecrow in the *Wizard of Oz* movie. Not stuffed with straw or anything. Just kind of lanky, like a rubbery old string bean. Ed Earl didn't impress me one way or the other. Skinny, pale, and blond. A kind of Pillsbury Doughboy, only not plump, just pasty. It was hard to tell how old he was. If he was my age, he was downright puny.

Pa-Daddy went around the room naming all of us for Steve and Ed Earl. Then he pointed at two chairs and told them to sit and have a bite.

"No thank you," Mr. Murdoch said. "We've already eaten. But you go ahead. Please don't let us interrupt."

Well, right off I noticed old Steve Murdoch didn't talk like us. I had him figured for a Yankee. Couldn't tell about Ed Earl, though, seeing as how he hadn't said a word.

"I finished my breakfast," I announced, hopping up from my chair. I beat feet for the door, hoping I could make a break for it before anybody tried to stop me.

Pa-Daddy was getting ready to crack a couple of eggs into the pan. "If you're going out, take Ed Earl, here, with you. He can show you around."

I felt my entire insides slide down into my bare feet. The last thing I wanted was to go traipsing around the countryside with the Pillsbury Pasteboy. So I didn't say anything, just headed for the door.

Next thing I knew, I was halfway down the porch steps with Ed Earl behind me. I couldn't tell how far behind me he was, but his shadow stretched almost all the way to mine.

"You don't need to come." I was getting pretty tired of this tracking game. "Pa-Daddy was being polite, that's all."

"I'm not following you." I could feel Ed Earl frowning at my back. "I'm headed down below to pick out some cypress knees. They just happen to be in this direction."

"Cypress knees?" I stopped short and spun around. Our noses almost collided. "You mean knees like this?" I pointed to my own knee, the one with the Mickey Mouse Band-Aid slapped across it.

Ed Earl thought about that for a minute. Then he dug his finger in his ear, like he hadn't heard me right. "Maybe."

"Maybe what?"

"I guess they look like that." He pointed to my knee. "Except without the Band-Aid."

"Maybe you're trying to be funny, Eddie, but you aren't."

He stood there staring at me, real thoughtful. "It's Ed Earl," he reminded me.

It suddenly occurred to me maybe he wasn't trying to be funny. Maybe he didn't have any sense of humor at all. "Fine. So show me these knees," I said, feeling a bit exasperated but a little curious, too.

Ed Earl headed for the stream behind our house. Then I followed him through some pastureland for a while.

"Where's your house?" I said as we walked along.

"About half a mile down the road from yours."

"Lived here long?"

"You mean in that house?" He kept picking up large sticks, inspecting them, and then tossing them aside till he found one he liked. Then he carried it alongside like it was a spear or something.

"Why? You live someplace else before?"

"Lots of places. But my mom was born and raised only a few miles from here."

"I figured you weren't from around here. I could tell right off."

Ed Earl stopped short and looked around, like he wasn't quite sure which way he wanted to go next. I waited real patient till he made up his mind, then followed right along. "So how long you lived in Florida?"

"Two years."

"In that house down the road?" I don't know what made me ask that, but somehow I had this feeling he hadn't lived there very long.

"That place?" I was beginning to think Ed Earl had the

attention span of a flea. He seemed to be trying to remember what we were talking about, as if he had his mind on more important things. "No. Just since January."

"Just you and your dad?"

"Yeah."

"What about your mom?" I knew it was none of my business, but I couldn't help myself. Seemed like I was always asking other kids about their moms. I don't know why. Maybe I wanted to find out if they had moms who did the kind of rotten stuff my mom did, or if I had the only one in the world.

"My mom's in Brazil," he said in this real flat voice. Then he wandered off to a nearby cypress pond and started stabbing his stick in the water.

It was about killing me not to ask more questions. Nanny Jo says when I get to asking folks things, I don't ever let up until they're about ready to blast me into the next county. But asking questions is what being a reporter is all about. And I wasn't getting much practice lately.

"Here's some good ones," Ed Earl said. He took his sneakers off and began rolling his jeans up to his knees. He had the skinniest, whitest legs I'd ever seen. Then the next thing I knew, he was wading around in the pond.

At least that got my attention long enough to stop asking questions. "You crazy, boy?" I yelled. "There's cottonmouths live in there."

Ed Earl held up his stick. I noticed it was forked at the

end. He probably figured he could pin down any old water snake that came his way. But it didn't matter if he *was* armed, because he wasn't getting me in that pond.

"Look." He pointed to a big twisted cypress tree with all these fat roots sticking up in a circle around it. They reminded me of those stalagmites I'd read about. Ed Earl patted one of them with the palm of his hand like it was some old stray dog he'd found. "This'll make a great lamp."

"Lamp?" I could feel some more questions bubbling and churning inside me, just waiting to pop out.

"Sure." He stuck his hand into the water. "I'll saw it off down here at the bottom."

I stared at that root, or stump, or whatever it was, for a second, and then it dawned on me, the top of it *did* look kind of like a knee.

"I'll have to come back for it later." He climbed out of the pond. "I don't have a saw with me." Then he picked up his sneakers and headed back toward the house.

"How you gonna make a lamp out of that?" I nodded back toward the cypress tree.

"Drill a hole, run a cord through it, slap a little varnish on it, and give it a lampshade." Ed Earl shrugged, as if he was saying, "Isn't that how everybody does it?"

"Then what?"

"Sell it."

"Sell it! Who'd be dumb enough to buy something like that?"

"Tourists."

"I don't see a sight lot of tourists around here," I told him.

"I take the lamps around to craft fairs and flea markets." He stopped to roll down his pant legs. "In the winter, when there are lots of tourists, I set up a roadside stand down by the highway. It's amazing what some people will buy when they're on vacation."

I'd about run out of questions on cypress-knee lamps. And I still wanted to ask Ed Earl about what his mom was doing in Brazil, but I kept hearing Nanny Jo's voice in my head saying, "Keep your nose out of other folks' business, and they'll keep theirs out of yours." Not that I had much interesting business anybody would want to know about.

When we got back to the house, Pa-Daddy was sitting on the front porch reading the newspaper. In Panther Ridge, all he had to do was walk out to the porch where the paper would be waiting for him. Now he had to drive clear to Bridgetown, which is about three miles from here, to get the morning news.

Louise was leaning against the railing, painting her fingernails some weird purple color. Ed Earl's pa had already left, so Ed Earl said he'd better head on home, too. I watched him hightailing it down to the road. For a skinny, pasty-faced kid, he moved pretty fast.

I wasn't in any mood to talk to Pa-Daddy, so I decided I'd see if there was any bacon left over from breakfast. Just as I reached for the doorknob, Rhonda Fay stomped onto the porch, flashlight in hand, and announced she had to go to the outhouse. Louise and I looked at each other. We knew Rhonda Fay was expecting one of us to escort her. Rhonda Fay won't set foot inside the outhouse until she does a spider check. The thing is, if she finds one, she makes somebody else kill it.

Rhonda Fay stood pointing the flashlight at me. Even though it was daytime, it was pretty dark in the outhouse. Downright impossible to hunt spiders without a light. "You can come with me," she announced, like she was doing me a big favor.

Louise jumped up, grabbed two empty buckets, and handed one to each of us. "You can bring back some creek water for the dishes while you're down there."

Rhonda Fay snapped up that old bucket like she was thinking of smacking Louise in the knee with it, then whipped around and stomped down the front stairs. I took the other bucket and followed along.

"What you going to do when I'm not around to kill those spiders?" I asked her.

"Get somebody else to do it."

"Louise won't go within ten thousand feet of any spider," I reminded her.

"Well, Pa-Daddy's home now." I could tell I was starting to get to her. The thing was, I was spoiling for a fight, but I wasn't sure why.

"Yeah, but he might get another job real soon. Then what?"

"Why don't you hush your mouth, Quinnella."

I hated it when she called me Quinnella. "You're going to have to face those old spiders one of these days, Rhonda Fay."

She stopped short and punched her fists into her waist. The bucket bounced against her hip. "Oh right. Just like you're going to be some famous reporter someday. Dream on."

"Shut your mouth. You don't know anything about it."

"I'll shut my mouth, if you shut up about those spiders."

"Fine," I said.

"Fine."

When we reached the outhouse, I took the flashlight and went in ahead of Rhonda Fay. Pa-Daddy had attached a regular toilet seat over the hole in the wood bench to make us feel more at home. Louise had added a basket with a bunch of her fashion magazines for general reading. I can't stand all that fashion junk. But the worst part was, she had plastered the wall with all these stinky stick-up air-freshener things. That powdery smell was enough to make me gag.

I flashed the light around a few times, then told Rhonda Fay it was all clear. Soon as she lowered her fanny onto the seat and I was backing out of the door, I flashed the light on the ceiling and screamed, "Whoa, how'd I ever miss that hideous old thing? Look, it's got fur!"

Rhonda Fay didn't even stop to pull her shorts back up.

She kind of tipped herself forward and lunged for the door. "Wha . . . what is it?" she shrieked.

"Can't tell." I flashed the light right in her eyes. "A bat, maybe."

"Well, don't just stand there, kill it!"

"You don't want to kill it, Rhonda Fay. It'll keep the mosquitoes out of there."

Rhonda Fay hiked her shorts back up. "How come you didn't see something that big the first time you looked?"

"Just didn't, that's all." I gave her my best innocent look.

Rhonda Fay narrowed her eyes and studied me for a minute. "There ain't no bat, Quinnella. You tried to trick me."

"Guess you're too darn smart for me, Rhonda Fay." I knew I was grinning up a storm, but I just couldn't help myself. With that she pounced on me like a cat on a cricket and started tearing at my hair. "I hate this place," she screamed into my ear.

We rolled sideways in the dirt. "Yeah, well I hate it, too."

"You're going to pay for this," she screamed, like somehow us having to live in this wilderness of weeds was all my fault.

"I didn't do anything," I said, pulling her off my head. "Cut it out, Rhonda Fay. You keep kicking up all this dirt, you'll ruin your sneakers."

Rhonda Fay backed off for a minute, stared down at her

feet, then kicked off her sneakers. I was in for it now. Rhonda Fay might be two years younger than me, but rassling with her is like rassling with a wounded panther. "Good Lord, can't you take a joke?" I said.

"Not if it ain't funny."

"You got an underdeveloped sense of humor, that's all." I was backing away a few feet at a time.

Rhonda Fay sidestepped into the outhouse. "If I didn't have to go so bad, I'd rearrange your teeth."

"Nice talk coming from a young lady," I said as she slammed the door. Rhonda Fay considers herself the only "lady" in the family, because of what she calls her good taste.

There didn't seem much point in hanging around waiting to get my teeth rearranged, so I snapped up my bucket and headed down to the creek.

In the distance, I could see one of the cypress ponds way out in the middle of the field. I got to wondering about Ed Earl and his cypress lamps. Just how much money would those tourists pay for one of those things? A lot, probably, on account of they didn't have anything like that back home. And I sure could use that money.

Then I got to thinking—a good fight with Rhonda Fay always seems to clear my head—maybe Ed Earl would show me how to make them, if I asked. All these ideas started buzzing around in my head like a mess of hungry mosquitoes. Maybe I could earn enough money to buy a computer. If I had a computer like the one we used at school, I could start my *own* newspaper. Course, I wasn't fooling myself. You can't run a computer without electricity. But we were bound to get some someday. Besides, maybe if I made enough money from selling those lamps, I could help Pa-Daddy pay for the electricity. It would be worth it.

I got to dreaming about maybe publishing a newspaper for kids my age. A newspaper that reported all the news in the county that kids would want to know about. And I'd be the publisher, editor, and reporter all rolled into one. So maybe my career as a journalist wasn't over after all. At least having a computer and my own newspaper would make swamp life a little more tolerable. I decided that as soon as I could, I'd go looking for Ed Earl and see if maybe we couldn't make some sort of business arrangement.

6

Big Trouble

The next day I had to postpone tracking down Ed Earl because it was Sunday. Every Sunday we all hop in the pickup and drive to the Baptist church near Nanny Jo Pearl's house. It's the same church Pa-Daddy has been going to ever since he was old enough to walk. Then after church, we always get together with some of the family for dinner at Nanny Jo's. Anyway, that's what we usually do. Except we'd already missed church the Sunday before on account of all that moving business. So it felt kind of good, getting back to the old routine.

Well, we'd no sooner parked the pickup and crossed the parking lot than dumb old pea-brained Mary Alice and two of her snotty friends came strolling up to me. Mary Alice looked so smug, you'd have thought she'd just won the lottery.

"If it isn't the Swamp Thing," she said, letting that stupid grin smear itself across her face. "Heard you folks gone backwoods."

I shot a glance Pa–Daddy's way. I'd told him this was going to happen. I mean, didn't I tell him the day we moved folks would start calling me the Swamp Thing? And I was right. But Pa–Daddy was already heading up the church steps with Louise and Rhonda Fay. Probably didn't hear a word Mary Alice said.

There was nothing to do but throw my head back and my chin out like I was above all of Mary Alice's petty foolishness and trot on after the others. Unfortunately, my exit was accompanied by Mary Alice and her friends chanting "Swamp Thing" behind me all the way to the front door.

Going to church is okay, I guess. I'm kind of used to it. Truth is, that morning it felt pretty good to be someplace that hadn't changed. Lots of the folks from Panther Ridge that had been scattered all over the county were there, so it felt nice and homey, almost like we'd never moved away.

I've never been good about sitting through those long sermons, though, so Pa–Daddy always lets me bring a little pad and a pencil, as long as I keep them low so no one notices. Sometimes I write about stuff I notice in church, like all that hair Sid Carruthers has growing out of his ears, and about how it must be hard for him to hear anything with that forest of fur plugging up his ear canals. Only that morning I felt like drawing instead of writing.

Rhonda Fay was sitting right next to me and kept wriggling around like she had chiggers in her drawers or something. Probably because Tanner McPherson was sitting across the aisle from her. I figured she was trying to get him to notice her.

Every now and then she'd look over to see what I was drawing. Mostly I'd been drawing cypress lamps—my own designs, of course, since I didn't have a clue what one looked like.

She poked her finger at my drawing. "That's one strange-looking mushroom," she whispered, bending over to get a good look, which is when I got a noseful of lilac water that about gagged me. For some dumb reason, Rhonda Fay always has to get herself all gussied up for church.

"This isn't a mushroom." I didn't need Rhonda Fay to remind me I didn't have one ounce of artistic talent.

"Well, what then?"

"Why should you care?" I wasn't much in the mood to explain cypress lamps to Rhonda Fay, especially since I wasn't all that sure what they were myself.

"Hush up." The voice came from somebody in the pew in front of us. And I knew just who it was, too. Mary Alice Taylor spun around so fast I thought she'd get whiplash. "This is the Lord's house." She was whispering, but somehow it sounded more like hissing. "Show some respect."

Me and Rhonda Fay both let out a little snort. Who

did Mary Alice think she was, telling *us* how to behave in church? Rhonda Fay went right back to her wriggling. But I was getting bored with my lamp drawings. I found myself staring at the back of Mary Alice's head. It was like I'd suddenly spotted a big target with a bull's-eye hanging there.

Reverend Bo Dillard was talking about the folks that had got laid off from the mines and how we shouldn't forget them in our prayers. Not that I was about to. He was halfway through his sermon when I got this urge. I don't know what got into me, but next thing I knew, I'd talked Rhonda Fay into letting me have her nail clippers. Rhonda Fay always carries nail clippers. She likes to keep her fingernails real short so no dirt can get under them. Her old mouth flopped open like a hooked fish when I leaned forward and snipped off a tiny end of Mary Alice's hair. I mean, Rhonda Fay's eyes about popped outta her head when she saw that.

But I couldn't help myself. Mary Alice had that glossy dark-brown hair of hers draped over the back of the pew like she was hanging it out to dry, and every now and then she would toss her head back a little, like she was trying to work the air through it real good. I took another snip, and me and Rhonda Fay watched the little brown bristles float to the floor.

Louise was sitting on the other side of me, but she was too busy watching her boyfriend, Lloyd, to notice I'd suddenly taken up hairdressing. Pa-Daddy was sitting next to Louise, and I could see his eyelids fluttering up and down, so I knew he was probably catching himself a late-morning nap.

Rhonda Fay really seemed to be enjoying this latest turn of events. Maybe because her own blond hair was thin as spider threads and only reached to the back of her training bra. Besides, Mary Alice had hardly taken her eyes off Tanner McPherson since he'd sat down. Course, right now, Tanner was too busy watching what *I* was doing to give one hoot about Mary Alice. He had that look on his face. You know, that look folks get when they're tending a tidy little brushfire and suddenly a big wind comes along and, whoosh, flames everywhere.

I took another snip of Mary Alice's hair, then tipped my chin toward Tanner, wearing my best pleased-as-punch look.

Rhonda Fay suddenly noticed that I was flirting with Tanner and decided she didn't like the direction this whole thing was taking. "There's gonna be trouble," she warned. "*Big* trouble." She tried to sound as solemn as she could, being in church and all, but I could tell by the smirk on her face that she was really looking forward to it. The "big trouble," that is.

I shrugged and went back to styling Mary Alice's hair. I clipped off three or four more strands—not long strands, just itty-bitty things—and slid my foot across the floor, sort of sweeping the hair under the pew, in case anybody noticed. Tanner McPherson looked like he was about ready to bust a gut, trying not to laugh out loud.

Rhonda Fay just sighed, like she could care less if Mary Alice left church bald that morning. As it turned out, I'd only managed a kind of zigzag pattern along the bottom before we all had to stand and sing "When the Roll Is Called Up Yonder."

"Your name sure ain't on that roll now," Rhonda Fay whispered, flexing her index finger in the direction of Mary Alice's hair. Then she tilted her nose toward the ceiling. Maybe she was looking for some angel of vengeance to swoop down on me.

"Who cares," I said. "Besides, it was worth it." The thing is, nobody—and I mean *nobody*—calls me the Swamp Thing and gets away with it.

Reverend Bo Dillard suddenly raised his hand like he was going to wave us all out of there, on account of he'd had enough of our foolishness for one morning. Then he gave the benediction and everyone started filing out. But me and Rhonda Fay made sure we hung around long enough to see Mrs. Taylor spin old Mary Alice around on her heels and ask if she'd gone and got the ends of her hair caught in the meat grinder again.

Course, that "*big* trouble" was bound to catch up with us sooner or later, but we were so busy laughing ourselves silly over the whole thing, we more or less forgot there would be heck to pay later. By the time we got to Nanny Jo's, we had pretty much put it to rest.

E.B. came wandering up to the truck as soon as Pa-Daddy pulled into the driveway. He pointed to the mountains of fried chicken and hot biscuits on the tables. "Help yourselves. Your Nanny Jo's been cooking since she got back from the early service this morning."

Eating was fine with me. The sooner we were finished, the sooner I could go climb around in the groves next to the house. Which was okay with E.B., because the picking season was over and we wouldn't be knocking any of the oranges off the trees.

Uncle Jeb and his new wife, Annie, and Great-aunt Reenie and her daughter, Jenny, and Jenny's husband, Sam, were already there sitting in the shade under the Australian pines where E.B. had set up the tables. When we got over there, I noticed everybody was talking about the new phosphate company that wanted to mine around the Pines. I'd almost forgot about Pa-Daddy mentioning it the day we went fishing. But hearing folks talking about it, I suddenly got that gnawing feeling in my belly again. The feeling that more bad news was hovering somewhere over our heads, just waiting its turn.

Great-aunt Reenie was going on about how if that company moved in, some of the folks would have to move out, because the new company would need most of the land in the area for mining. I started thinking about how some of the Panther Ridge folks had just barely set their new-bought houses on cinder blocks in the Pines. Lots of those folks are my friends, kids I grew up with, kids I went to school with.

I was just about to ask if anybody knew what would happen to Nanny Jo and E.B.'s land, when Uncle Jeb suddenly turned to Pa-Daddy and changed the subject.

"How about them closing down the mines up there in Panther Ridge. Guess that don't bode well for you, big brother." Uncle Jeb leaned back and patted his fat belly like he had just downed a satisfying meal, which he hadn't, because nobody had eaten anything yet.

Pa-Daddy had already informed us we didn't need to go mentioning to the family that he had been laid off. So I wasn't prepared for Uncle Jeb suddenly announcing it to the whole world like that. Uncle Jeb is Pa-Daddy's younger brother. He got himself married to Annie Polhemus a few months ago and thinks he's pretty big stuff since now he runs her Laundromat for her. Up until then about all he did was watch TV and build little forts out of Popsicle sticks.

Pa-Daddy slid himself into a lounge chair next to the table and stared up at the pine branches overhead. "There's been layoffs before. Probably just temporary. Besides, if this other mining company comes in, it could mean jobs for folks."

Uncle Jeb gave him a sly look. I could tell he wanted to

see Pa-Daddy squirm. Jeb's always had a mean streak in him. "What you going to do in the meantime?"

But Pa-Daddy looked him right in the eye, cool as chipped ice. "Same as we always do. Get by."

By this time, everybody had eased over to where Pa-Daddy and Jeb were talking so they wouldn't miss anything. Families are like that. They got to be where the drama is. And if there isn't enough drama to suit them, well, then, they'll just help it along. Like Great-aunt Reenie, who was leaning in so close, she was about to tip over. Right off she had to say, "Maybe Jeb here could give you work at the Laundromat."

Rhonda Fay grabbed my wrist. Hard. "Let's get something to eat. I'm half starved to death."

I figured Rhonda Fay wasn't really about to keel over from starvation. She just didn't want to stay there and watch Pa-Daddy get himself humiliated. Neither did I. So we started filling our plates when, right about then, E.B. wandered over and said, "Claude, boy, I need some advice on that old smokehouse over yonder." He wagged his leathery finger in the direction of the building he was talking about. "Thinking of fixing it up. Got a minute to take a look before dinner?"

Pa-Daddy looked up at E.B. like he was the cavalry itself come to rescue him, which wasn't all that far from the truth.

Pa-Daddy stretched to his feet, and that little circle of

folks spread out to let him and E.B. pass by. I knew E.B. didn't need advice on the smokehouse. Fact is, everybody there knew they were going to the smokehouse to get themselves a cold drink. The smokehouse is where E.B. keeps a laundry tub full of ice and cans of beer whenever he's got company.

Nanny Jo, being a good Baptist, won't have anyone drinking in her house, or anyplace else on her land. But E.B. figures it wouldn't be very hospitable of him if he couldn't offer a drink to his guests now and then, so he always has a few hidden out in the smokehouse. That old smokehouse hasn't been used for anything else but E.B.'s secret hiding place ever since he came to live there four years ago.

We didn't see much of Pa-Daddy the rest of the afternoon, but when it came time to go, E.B. drove our pickup, with Nanny Jo following in her old green '64 Nova. The Nova is Nanny Jo's first and only car. She didn't learn how to drive till she was near sixty. And even though she did okay with a stick shift, she never could get the hang of putting it in reverse. When we lived in Panther Ridge, she always made Pa-Daddy back the car out of our driveway for her and set it facing forward, so she could drive home. She wouldn't even back out of her own driveway. Instead, she'd kind of worn a circle in her front yard over the years.

We'd all pretty much figured out that Pa-Daddy wasn't in any condition to drive. And Nanny Jo didn't look at all pleased about it, either. Louise and Rhonda Fay had climbed into the front seat before I even got to the truck, so I was stuck riding in the back with Pa-Daddy.

It was an empty, strange feeling, driving past the turnoff for Panther Ridge, knowing we weren't going that direction anymore. In the old days, we would have been almost home by now. Instead, we still had a long way to go before we got to the Swamp House, which is what me and Rhonda Fay had recently taken to calling our place.

We were coming up to the old turnoff, but Pa-Daddy didn't even seem to notice. He was busy belting out an Elvis song about being his "teddy bear." He tried to get me to sing along, like we always used to, but I wasn't in a singing mood. In the old days, when we were buddies, we sang together all the time. I know the words to every Elvis Presley song ever recorded.

Truth is, Pa-Daddy does a pretty good impression of Elvis when he's in the right mood, which he certainly was after all those trips to the smokehouse. And whenever he forgets the words, he just makes up his own silly verses. Mom used to sing along with him too, making up her own crazy words. They'd always try to outdo each other. Personally, I always thought Mom's verses were the funniest. I wondered if Pa-Daddy remembered him and Mom singing like that.

He stopped singing finally and rested his head against the back window. Then with no warning at all, he said, "E.B. offered me a job."

"No kidding. That's great!"

Pa-Daddy shook his head. "It'd be like taking a handout."

"Pa-Daddy," I said. "It's not a handout. You'd be working for pay."

Pa-Daddy tipped his cap forward to shade his eyes. "There's another reason," he said. "I don't mind working for E.B., but those are Nanny Jo's groves."

"So?" I was really getting confused.

"I know this is hard for you to understand, honey. But the truth is, I can't go back there. That old woman will be trying to run my life. And I couldn't take that. Not right now."

"Pa-Daddy, it's a job."

But he just shook his head. "To my way of thinking, if it hadn't been for Nanny Jo, maybe my life would have turned out different. Maybe I could have been a basketball star."

Well, that was pretty surprising news considering I didn't even know Pa-Daddy had ever played basketball. "I've never seen you play basketball," I said, trying my best to sound civil. "Where'd you get such an idea?"

"Made junior varsity when I was a freshman in high school." He eased himself against the cab of the truck and pillowed the back of his head with his hands. "I was good, too. Real good."

"Well, what happened?" In spite of myself, I could feel my body settling in for one of Pa-Daddy's stories. Pa-

Daddy's stories are about the next best thing to TV when it comes to entertainment.

"Nothing. I quit, that's all."

Right then I knew this wasn't going to be one of his stories. "Why?"

"Nanny Jo." He practically whispered her name, as if she might hear him if he said it too loud.

"What's Nanny Jo got to do with you not being a basketball star?" I asked him.

Pa-Daddy raked his hand through that unruly red hair of his, then shook his head. "You ain't going to believe this, but that old woman wouldn't let me wear my uniform. She said exposing naked legs clear to the thigh for the entertainment of the general population was about as sinful as a person could get. She made me wear overalls. Do you believe that! I had to play basketball in my overalls. Overalls!" He kept saying it over again like he couldn't quite believe it himself.

My backside was getting sore from bouncing along in the pickup. I tried kneeling for a while, but that didn't help much. "But you could still play, couldn't you?"

"In overalls? Sure. But I wasn't gonna make a fool of myself. So I quit the team. Not one soul in that whole school ever let me forget about them overalls, either."

The truck hit a bump and Pa-Daddy lowered his hands to steady himself. "Didn't matter none. I was pretty bored with school by then, anyway. Dropped out before my last year."

"Sorry to hear that. About the overalls, I mean." I already knew he'd never finished high school. The whole family knew it. So that part wasn't a surprise. And I could see why he'd never told any of us the overalls story.

"Now do you understand?" he asked.

"About what?"

Pa-Daddy puffed out his cheeks like some big old walrus. "Nanny Jo's always trying to tell me what to do. If I went to work for her, it'd be a whole lot worse. Downright intolerable."

Pa-Daddy stared up at the sky for a time, like he was expecting to find something there. "Nothing ever turns out the way we think, Quinn. Remember that." He gave me a warning look. I noticed his eyes were bloodshot. "Best not to make any definite plans about things. Somebody or something always comes along and rearranges them for you."

"Why don't you just tell E.B. how you feel?" I said. "Maybe he can talk to Nanny Jo about it."

He started in singing "Hard Headed Woman" then. I knew he was just teasing me because I was being stubborn about this Nanny Jo thing. But let's face it. A job's a job. Anyway, I didn't join in. I guess you could say me and Pa-Daddy just weren't singing the same tune these days. Besides, it was too tempting to change the lyrics to "hard headed man," which might not have set too well with him right then.

I mean, there he was, talking about folks coming along

and rearranging your affairs, like it or not, and all I could think of was how he'd rearranged mine. Well, maybe he thought he could run my life now, but he couldn't do it forever. I started clenching my jaw so hard, I was afraid I'd wind up with a mouthful of splintered teeth. Well, I sure wasn't going to end up flopping around in the back of some old pickup drunk on beer and whining about how somebody else messed up my life. No sir. I already had my own plans. Big plans for my future. And nobody, not even Pa-Daddy, was going to stop me.

Ed Earl

By the time we turned into the dirt road leading to our house, all I could think about was Ed Earl and those cypress lamps and making money to buy a computer. Pa-Daddy was catching himself forty winks, even though being bumped about in the back of the pickup isn't all that great for sleeping. But I was glad he was asleep so I didn't have to talk to him anymore.

Suddenly, there was Ed Earl, ambling along up ahead. Even with his back to us I could see he was carrying one of those cypress knees. I pounded my fist on the rear window of the pickup to get E.B.'s attention. "Hey," I shouted, "stop the truck!"

"What for?" he yelled back.

"I need to talk to Ed Earl a minute."

E.B. pulled up right next to Ed Earl, who was shuffling

along like he had all the time in the world. You would have thought he was ninety years old, the way he moved.

"Hey," said Ed Earl, when he spotted us.

"Hey, yourself." I climbed out of the pickup. "I'm walking with Ed Earl," I announced to E.B. He got this sly old grin on his face. I knew he was figuring I was sweet on Ed Earl, but I didn't care. I had more important things to think about.

E.B. leaned out the window and actually winked at me. It was downright embarrassing. "Enjoy your walk," he said, then took off down the road.

"Nice cypress knee," I said when we were alone.

Ed Earl nodded, like he already knew that, and kept on walking. Course, I knew from our last hike down to the cypress pond that he wasn't much on conversation, so it didn't really bother me, him not saying much and all.

We got as far as my house and Ed Earl stopped. I guess he figured this was where I was getting off. Funny thing was, he hadn't once asked me why I'd started walking with him in the first place. I wondered if maybe there wasn't a single curious bone in his whole entire body. Naturally, me being the queen of questions, it was pretty hard to imagine anybody not wanting to know about everything there was to know . . . and then some.

Ed Earl turned to go. "See ya."

"Can you show me how to make those lamps?" I blurted it right out because in another minute he'd be gone and I hadn't even brought up the subject yet.

He shrugged like it was no big deal. "Sure."

"Now?"

"You mean right now?"

"Why not? Now's as good a time as any. We still got a couple hours before it gets dark."

Ed Earl set the cypress knee in the dirt by his foot. I guess he was getting tired of carrying it around. He kept staring down at it like he was afraid it'd run off. But I could tell he was puzzling over what I'd said.

"I guess it's okay."

I could hear Louise singing some stupid country-western song on the front porch. Fact is, the whole county could probably hear Louise singing. She always sings like she's onstage at the Grand Ole Opry in Nashville with ten thousand folks looking on. It was downright unseemly, her up there bellowing out all this gushy romantic junk.

"I'm going over to Ed Earl's," I shouted at the top of my lungs, so she could hear me over the singing.

Louise nodded and waved, and never missed a beat.

———

Ed Earl's house was like nothing I'd ever set eyes on before. I wasn't even sure it was a house. When I finally got it figured out, I realized it was an old mobile home with a couple extra rooms built on.

It turned out him and his dad had plumbing and electricity on account of something called a generator, which didn't seem fair. But then I got to thinking maybe I could earn enough money to buy us one, and I started feeling a little better.

Ed Earl's room didn't look anything like a place folks would sleep in. He had these posters all over the wall. Not rock stars like most kids have, but posters like one that showed all the constellations. And there was one that had all these funny letters and numbers that Ed Earl said were symbols for different chemical elements like hydrogen and helium and stuff.

I pointed to one of the posters. "Who's that old guy whose hair looks like he got his finger stuck in a light socket?"

Ed Earl stared at me like he couldn't figure out if I was serious or not. "Albert Einstein. He was a genius. He developed the theory of relativity."

"Yeah? Well, I got a few theories of my own about relatives."

I could see he was getting pretty disgusted with me. "It's a joke, Ed Earl. I was making a joke." Truth is, I didn't know anything about Albert Einstein or his dumb old theory, but I sure didn't want Ed Earl to know that. "What's all this stuff for, anyway?" I figured this was a good time to change the subject.

Ed Earl picked up a rock and started turning it over and over again in his hands. "Nothing. It's interesting, that's all."

I could see he thought it was pretty interesting, because everywhere I looked there were shelves filled with all

79

kinds of rocks, and shells, and tiny animal bones. There was even an old kitchen table sitting in the middle of the room. Since it was pretty near buried under books and junk, I figured Ed Earl used it as a desk.

"You thinking about being some kind of scientist?"

"Maybe."

"Well, that's a pretty good job, I hear."

"My dad's a biochemist," he said out of the blue. Then he put the rock back on the shelf like he didn't want to talk about that, like he was maybe sorry he'd brought it up.

"So what's a biochemist do?" I tried to sound like I wasn't all that interested, so he wouldn't think I was being nosey.

"Most of them work in labs for big corporations, but my dad doesn't work in a lab. He teaches at a university not far from here." Ed Earl stood there twisting his yellow-white hair around his finger, looking kind of thoughtful. I figured he had said about all he was going to say. But then out popped this little sigh. "He isn't teaching right now. He's taking time off to write a book." He turned his back to me and began running his fingers over the rocks and bones real gentle. "My mom's in Brazil with this team of scientists. They're doing research on the rain forest."

I couldn't help wondering if maybe Ed Earl's mom had gone to Brazil like my mom had gone on tour with the bluegrass band. I wondered if her letters had gotten fewer and fewer. Was he only getting postcards these days? Did she make it back for his birthday? Would Mr. Murdoch get a long letter from her one day saying how she really loved him and Ed Earl but . . .

"When's she coming back?" I asked him. That was one question I would never stop asking myself.

Ed Earl shrugged. "I guess she'll be home by Christmas. She's got to be back in time to teach at the university next spring. My dad, too. He's supposed to have his book finished by late fall so he can go back to teaching in January."

I felt bad for Ed Earl. I could tell this whole arrangement didn't suit him one bit. Still, at least *his* mom was coming home.

"Where *is* your dad, anyway?" I glanced around like I was expecting him to hop right out of the closet or something.

"I don't know. Probably out walking." He picked up a pencil from the table and began drumming with it. He was getting fidgety. "My dad goes for walks a lot. He says he does his best thinking when he's walking."

"He sure did a lot of interesting things with this old mobile home," I said, nodding and looking around.

Ed Earl frowned and shook his head. "My dad didn't do any of this. This was my granddad Duvane's place." He wandered over to the window and leaned his forehead against the screen, like he was thinking real serious about something. "I'm named after him," he said after a few minutes. "He was my mom's dad. When he died he left this land and everything on it to my folks, but we never stayed here. We'd pretty much forgotten all about the place, till my dad needed someplace quiet to work. Someplace that wouldn't cost us anything."

Somehow he didn't look too happy when he said that. I guess it had to be pretty lonely for him out here. At least I had Louise and Rhonda Fay. Even if they weren't good company, I could always find some new and interesting way to get on their nerves, which helped to pass the time.

"So where do you make the lamps?" I asked, trying to change the subject. I could see Ed Earl was feeling pretty down.

"In the shed. I'll show you." He practically leaped for the door. I guess maybe he was glad to be back talking about something he had some control over. I knew just how he felt.

I followed him outside. In back of the house was this shed made all of tin. Tin sides, tin roof . . . and no windows. At least I didn't think so, but then Ed Earl went inside and, with big wooden poles, propped open these tin flaps on either side of the room. As far as I was concerned, it was an open invitation to every mosquito in the county to step inside and help himself to a free lunch.

It was so hot in there, I could hardly breathe. Since there weren't any lights, it was hard to see, especially with the sun about to set. But I could tell without looking that there wasn't any floor, only hard-packed dirt.

Ed Earl spread out his arms like he was going to give

the room a big hug. "My granddad built this. He used to call it his tinkering shop. It's not a half-bad place to work. A little hot, maybe."

The workbench was right in front of one of the make-shift windows, so I figured there was probably enough light for him to work by during the day. Shelves with boxes of wire on them—and stuff I didn't know the names of—were all around the walls. About a dozen finished cypress lamps were stacked on some other shelves. Since I'd never seen one before, I didn't know what to expect. But it turned out they looked pretty nice, considering they were made out of old cypress knees.

Ed Earl didn't waste any time getting down to business. "You've got to figure start-up costs, first," he said.

"What's that?"

He began ticking things off on his fingers. "Well, you have to buy the wire, the fixtures that hold the lightbulbs, the varnish, and when you're all done, the lampshades."

"So what's it gonna cost me?"

Ed Earl thought a minute. "About fifteen dollars a lamp."

"What?" I guess I wasn't expecting to plunk down a whole lot of money till the business got going. "Do I look like Mrs. Rockefeller to you? Do you see hundred-dollar bills jumping out of my pockets?"

He shrugged. "You asked. I'm just telling you what it costs."

"How much you make selling one of those things?"

"Fifty dollars, usually. That's a thirty-five-dollar profit."

"I know how much of a profit it is. I can do math." And I was doing plenty of multiplying in my head right then, trying to figure how much money I could make if I made ten lamps over the next few weeks. Naturally, I couldn't help but think about how long it would take me to save up for my computer.

Then old Ed Earl piped up and said, "Of course, you have to take fifteen dollars of that profit and invest it in the next lamp."

"That's only a twenty-dollar profit on each lamp." I guess I sounded pretty disappointed. Especially considering I'd been dreaming up big plans for that money.

Ed Earl picked up one of the lamps and handed it to me. I guess he wanted me to get a closer look. "Twenty dollars is still a good profit. It doesn't take that long to make the lamps once you get the hang of it."

"Yeah. Well, I just don't happen to have fifteen dollars to invest right now." I handed the lamp back to him.

I guess I must have looked pretty down about the whole thing, because right then Ed Earl said, "Well, I've been thinking about getting an assistant. Someone to do the varnishing. I can't pay much, maybe two dollars a lamp."

Right away I started figuring how many lamps I'd have to varnish before I'd have my fifteen dollars. It didn't sound all that bad. Besides, while I did the varnishing, I could watch Ed Earl and learn how to make the lamps.

"Okay. It's a deal." I stuck out my hand. Ed Earl stood there like he wasn't sure what to do with it. Finally I grabbed his hand and gave it a good shake, so he'd know I meant business.

Suddenly I heard this loud clap of thunder. It sounded like somebody was pounding on the tin roof with a hammer. When I stuck my head out the door, I knew why it had gotten so dark in the shed. A storm was brewing. And it was coming up fast.

8

Storms

I didn't stop running till I was clear out of sight of Ed Earl's house. You'd have thought a wild panther was on my tail. When I finally stopped to catch my breath, I felt like I'd just stepped out of the creek. I was soaking wet from head to toe. Bugs hit my skin and stuck there.

The air was so still and wet, I could hardly breathe. It was coming. I could hear it rumbling through the trees. Storms are like that. They can come up on you real sudden sometimes. One minute everything's as sunny as can be, and the next thing you know, the sky's the color of a dirty old nickel. That's when the real thundering begins. The kind you can feel shoot up through the soles of your feet and thump in your chest.

When the first flash of lightning skittered across the sky, I took off running again. I was still a good quarter mile from home. I knew better than to take shelter under a tree. But I got to admit, running right down the middle of the road didn't thrill me much, either. All I kept thinking was, "Please, God, don't let that lightning hit me."

The lightning was getting worse. You would have thought somebody was up in those clouds shooting electric arrows right to the ground. Suddenly I felt my scalp twitch. My hair was practically standing on end. I dropped to the ground, curled myself into a ball, and covered my head. I knew it was near. Real near. But I kept myself all rolled up. Then came the crack. It was louder than any shotgun I'd ever heard.

When the roots of my hair stopped tingling, I got up the nerve to take a peek. There I was, kneeling in the dirt like I was saying my prayers, and only a few yards away, laying on the side of the road, was almost half a tree. The other half, and part of the stump, were still standing, charred and smoking like a chimney fire. That old lightning bolt had split the tree right down the middle and blown the bark right off. My whole body went limp. I felt like I didn't have a single muscle left to get myself to my feet, let alone all the way home.

The rain came then, so hard I couldn't see anything in front of me. It slanted right into my face, stinging my eyes. I was shaking all over, but I knew I had to get home. I was more scared than I'd ever been in my entire life, but this was no time to sit down and whine. I made myself crawl a few feet forward, afraid my legs wouldn't support me, but finally I pulled myself up and began to run as fast as I could.

By the time I reached the open meadow where our house was, my lungs felt as if somebody had pumped them full of scorching-hot air. In the distance, I could make out Louise standing on the front porch holding a kerosene lantern. It about scared me to death to run across that open meadow, but there wasn't anything else to do. Noplace else to take shelter. I would have to meet that storm head-on.

I hit our front steps at top speed, landing like one of those sprinters in the Olympics. Louise set down the lantern and grabbed me by the shoulders. She stood there pinching my collarbone with her fingers, till it downright hurt.

"A field mouse has got more sense than you," she said, digging her fingers in deeper. "We all thought you'd stay on at Ed Earl's till the storm was over."

I wriggled out from under her grasp. "There wasn't much of a storm when I headed out. It came up real sudden."

A crash of thunder caught our attention, and we both spun around just as this burst of lightning washed the meadow in an eerie silver light.

From inside the house, somebody who sounded pretty angry shouted, "Claude Ellerbee, I been trying to track you down all afternoon. You just take off for some god-forsaken place and don't tell nobody where you're moving. Don't install no phone. No wonder your younguns don't act like natural folks."

"Mrs. Taylor and Mary Alice are inside." Louise sounded real matter-of-fact about it all, but I could tell she was waiting to see my reaction to the news.

I kept my eyes on the meadow. I wasn't about to give her the satisfaction of knowing I found the situation pretty unnerving. Truth is, I'd been so busy running for my life, I passed right by the Taylors' old station wagon without even seeing it. Seemed like that "*big* trouble" had caught up to us sooner than Rhonda Fay and me had expected.

Louise grabbed a fistful of my hair and began wringing it dry like it was a piece of soggy laundry. "Better come inside and get them wet things off."

"*Those* wet things," I said. I had to find some way to stall for time, and picking on old Louise seemed as good as anything else.

Louise dropped my hair and folded her arms. "Well, if it ain't the grammar police." She let out a huffy little snort. "Try listening to yourself sometime. That don't exactly sound like the Queen's English rolling off your tongue."

"Well, at least I'm trying," I said.

"Oh, you're trying, all right. Very trying." She gave my hair another wringing.

I jerked my head away from her hand. "I think I'll stay out here for a while. Already been through one bad storm tonight."

Louise acted like what I had to say didn't matter a bit, which wasn't anything new. "Well, with all that practice, you should be good and ready to face the next one." Taking charge, she spun me around on my heels, shoved me through the front door, and pushed me through the living room all the way to the kitchen.

Mrs. Taylor stopped shouting so she could see who it was being rude enough to come barging in on her right in the middle of all her yelling. Except for Mrs. Taylor's false eyelashes, her and Mary Alice were practically dressed alike, both of them wearing T-shirts from Sea World and faded blue jeans.

The two kerosene lanterns sent these shadows scurrying up the wall, making everything look creepier than usual. Mrs. Taylor was already spooky enough without the shadows flickering on her face.

"This one," she snapped, wagging a finger at me, "this one's got serious problems."

Louise handed me a towel, and I pretended I was too busy drying off to notice Mrs. Taylor was talking about me.

Rhonda Fay was parked on top of the kitchen table. Every now and then she wet her finger and wiped an imaginary smudge off her sneakers. I couldn't be sure if she was listening to Mrs. Taylor or not.

Pa-Daddy was leaning against the stove like he was trying to get himself warm. He had his arms folded across his chest real tight. "What've you got to say for yourself, Quinn?"

"About what?"

"About this haircutting business." Pa-Daddy wasn't looking too good. I figured he was probably feeling a little poorly on account of all those trips to the smokehouse at Nanny Jo's earlier.

I jerked my chin toward Mary Alice, whose face was so red and swollen I thought maybe a big old bee had stung her right on both her cheeks. "She's dreaming. I never touched her old hair."

"That's a lie!" Mary Alice screamed, starting to cry all over again. "She was sitting right behind me in church. I sat down in the pew with my hair looking perfectly fine, and I got up looking like somebody had attacked it with pinking shears."

"We don't own no pinking shears," Rhonda Fay volunteered, managing to look both bored and disgusted at the same time. Actually she sounded pretty convincing. I had to admit, when the chips were down, you could always count on Rhonda Fay. I mean, Rhonda Fay and me might have our own personal ongoing feuds, but when it comes to defending family, the rule is we always stick together.

Pa-Daddy turned to me. "You want to explain yourself, Quinnella?"

I gave Pa-Daddy a puzzled look. "Explain what?"

"Explain this," Mrs. Taylor shrieked, spinning Mary Alice around so I could get a good look at her hair.

"That's a real interesting hairstyle you got there, Mary Alice. Where'd you have it done?"

"You know darn well where I had it done!"

"Where?" I raised my eyebrows in one of my surprised, innocent looks.

"*You* did it, you psychopath, that's what!"

"Quinn's a little high-spirited, maybe," Louise said angrily, "but she ain't no psychopath."

Mrs. Taylor slid her shoulder bag down her arm and slammed it on the kitchen table, then took to pointing that wagging finger of hers at Pa-Daddy. "I've had about enough of this. I'll tell you straight out, Claude Ellerbee, this is only the beginning. If you don't put a stop to this deviant behavior now . . . well, there's just no telling. Maybe y'all better have Quinn here locked up in a mental institution while there's still time. Maybe right now it's scissors or whatever. But Lord knows, a year from now it'll be knives, then axes."

"Then chain saws," Mary Alice said, being helpful.

"Nobody will be safe." Mrs. Taylor collapsed into a nearby chair. One of those false eyelashes of hers was starting to come unglued at the corner.

Louise took a few cautious steps toward Mrs. Taylor. "Can I get you anything? A glass of water?"

But Mrs. Taylor was too busy staring me down to hear Louise. I stared her right back. "You know what you

92

done," Mrs. Taylor told me. "Now you got to make good on it."

"How you make good on somebody's hair? Glue it back on?" I said, trying to look thoroughly annoyed. "I'm not saying I did it. I just want to know."

"You make good by paying for a decent haircut. That's how." Mrs. Taylor began to sound a bit calmer. "And then you can start praying to the Lord for forgiveness."

I hopped up on the table beside Rhonda Fay, pulled my legs up, and crossed them. I sat there smack in the middle of that old kitchen table, my eyes half closed, pretending like I was communicating with ancient spirits.

Mrs. Taylor sucked in air between her clenched teeth. "Well?"

"Now, I'm not saying I did it," I reminded everybody. "But it sure is a painful sight having to look at Mary Alice's ugly hair. So, being a friend of Mary Alice's, I'm willing to donate a little something to help her get a decent haircut."

Out of the corner of my eye, I saw Pa-Daddy shaking his head. I couldn't tell if it was because he was mad or because he couldn't believe what he was hearing. "I think you better apologize to Mary Alice," he said.

I stared up at him like he'd gone and sold me to a band of passing Gypsies. How could he let me down like that? Families were supposed to stick together.

I looked around for reinforcements, but Rhonda Fay had quietly slid off the table and was helping Louise put on the coffeepot while Louise cut up slices of her most recent experiment, apple-cinnamon cake, for everybody. Since when did my family take to celebrating my humiliation?

I wanted to tell Pa-Daddy how Mary Alice had called me the Swamp Thing. But I didn't think he'd much care.

Louise took a carton of milk from the ice chest and put a cold glass of milk and a thick slice of cake in front of Mary Alice, like some dumb peace offering. I wanted to strangle her. Instead, I hopped off the table and slammed through the swinging door into the living room. Nobody was going to make me apologize to Mary Alice. Not after she'd gone and called me the Swamp Thing.

Pa-Daddy was right on my heels. I felt his heavy hand come down on my shoulder. "Stop right there, Quinnella," he said, pushing me into a nearby chair. My mouth curled itself into a nasty sneer. I didn't even feel bad about the way he looked, kind of lost and confused, standing there with his hands spread out, palms up, in front of him.

"What's going on here?" he asked. "I need to know why you been acting like this."

"Like what?"

"Don't you go taking that tone with me, Quinnella. You know darn well what I'm talking about. You ain't been behaving like yourself for weeks now."

"Yeah? And just what am I supposed to behave like?"

"Like yourself."

"This is myself. I'm behaving just the way myself would behave."

Pa-Daddy puffed out his cheeks and let out this exasperated sigh. He ran his fingers through his sweaty hair and sat down across from me. We were eyeball to eyeball. "If you don't want to talk to me about what's bothering you, that's your business. But whether you like it or not, you're going to march out there and apologize to Mary Alice."

I gripped the arms of the chair and leaned forward. "I hate this place, this ugly old Swamp House," I said through clenched teeth. "And I hate this whole family."

Pa-Daddy was shaking all over like he had the fever or something. For a minute I thought he might actually hit me, which is something he'd never done. Instead, he just stood up and walked back to the kitchen, leaving me to stew in my own orneriness.

9

Deadwood

Louise evened up Mary Alice's hair for her that very same night, the night of "the incident." Louise has had a lot of practice on all of us, especially on Pa-Daddy, so she's pretty good at haircutting. I figure if she doesn't get a job as a game-show hostess she can always be a hairdresser.

Pa-Daddy about drove me crazy until I finally apologized to Mary Alice before her and her mother left the house. Course, what I ended up saying was, "Sorry about your hair, Mary Alice, but to my way of thinking, it's an improvement," which is about the best anyone could expect from me under the circumstances.

Me and Pa-Daddy didn't have much to say to each other after that. Not that we'd been doing all that much talking, anyway. The other thing was, I couldn't help thinking the situation would be a whole lot different if Mom was here. She'd know just what to say to Pa-Daddy to get him to take that job tending Nanny Jo's groves. She'd probably even find a way to make us feel okay about living in the swamp.

That's when I decided to break Pa-Daddy's rule about not writing or calling her. We didn't have a phone, but that didn't mean I couldn't write her a postcard or something. So I dug around in the kitchen drawer and found some old postcards from our trip to Sea World a few years back. I picked one that had this picture of three dolphins leaping into the air, getting ready to jump through these big hoops.

From: Quinnella Ellerbee
        The Swamp House
        Nowhere, Florida

Dear Mom,
   Maybe you're busy with your new career and all, but me and Louise and Rhonda Fay sure could use a little advice about Pa-Daddy. He just isn't himself these days. Could you please write and tell us what to do? You can write to us at Nanny Jo's so Pa-Daddy won't find out. We don't have a telephone.

                    Your Daughter,
                    Quinnella

TO:
Bonnie Ellerbee
c/o Riverside Tavern
U.S. Highway 10
Mobile, AL 36600

p.s. We don't have electricity or plumbing either!

All I needed was Mom's address. The last one we had was for Mobile, Alabama. That's where her band was playing when she wrote Pa-Daddy the divorce letter. I figured even if she'd moved on, maybe she'd left a forwarding address with the post office. Anyway it was worth a try. So I sat down and wrote to her that very day.

Then I turned the card over and wrote our names—mine, Louise's, and Rhonda Fay's—one on each of the dolphins. I don't know why. I guess it was a pretty weird thing to do. But I did it anyway.

A few days later, I hitched a ride to Bridgetown with Ed Earl and his dad, and while they were shopping for groceries, I went straight to the post office and mailed my postcard. While I was standing there in front of that "out-of-town" mail slot holding my postcard, I started wondering if maybe I should have written Mom a whole letter. I sure had a lot of stuff to tell her, about moving to the swamp, and Ed Earl, and my business plans. I thought she'd like hearing about me planning my own newspaper.

But the thing was, she was the one who left us. And so, to my way of thinking, she didn't deserve a whole letter. Besides, a postcard didn't seem as bad as a letter when it came to breaking Pa-Daddy's rule. I mean it's just a little old innocent card, right? Anyway the postcard was getting all sweaty in my hand, so I finally mailed it. I just dropped it in that dumb slot, right along with all my hopes.

By now me and Ed Earl were going cypress-knee hunting almost every morning. Since there were two of us, we managed to stack up about a dozen more of those knees by the end of the week. Ed Earl said he would pay me extra for helping him in the cypress swamp and for carrying some of the knees back to his workshop.

The only really good thing that happened that week was that Pa-Daddy and his old buddy Joe Whiggs, who had also got laid off, finally put a manual pump on the well outside. Then they ran a pipe to the kitchen and rigged up another hand pump by the sink. We wouldn't have to go running down to the creek to fetch water anymore. Course, it wasn't like we had hot-and-cold running water. Just plain icy-cold well water that had to be heated up every time we wanted to wash something. But it was still better than carrying those buckets back and forth, and taking baths in the creek.

Anyway, this morning me and Ed Earl were coming back from one of our hunts, and by the time we reached the meadow, my arms were getting tired from carrying a cypress knee. I set it down and wiped the sweat from my forehead. "Let's stop by my house for a drink of water," I said. "We can take these over to your place later."

Ed Earl said that was fine with him. So I picked up my cypress knee and we took off again. But just as we were heading up to the house, here came Pa-Daddy hightailing it down the road, going so fast he didn't even notice us standing by the side of the ditch. He shot into our meadow in his pickup, heading toward the house like he had a herd of stampeding buffalo behind him. He didn't even keep that truck on the driveway. Not that two dirt ruts make much of a road, but Pa-Daddy had pretty much decided to keep using the same spot till he wore it down into a regular driveway.

When me and Ed Earl got to the house, we found Louise sitting on the front porch drinking iced tea and eating boiled peanuts, which was about the only snacking food we got these days. Joe Whiggs had given Pa-Daddy a mess of raw peanuts from his peanut patch, and Louise boiled them up for us.

"Your dad's been looking for you," Louise said to Ed Earl. He nodded, but instead of turning on his heels and heading home, he sat down on the porch step and helped himself to a couple of peanuts, like he planned to stay awhile.

"Nanny Jo been by today?" I asked her.

"You expecting Nanny Jo?" she said.

"I just wondered if she came by, that's all."

"Well, she hasn't," Louise said, giving me a funny look. "Why?"

I shrugged and popped a peanut in my mouth. "Just wondered." I wasn't about to tell Louise about the postcard I'd sent to Mom, or that I was expecting a letter from her any day.

Louise took the bowl of peanuts from my lap where I'd been hogging it. "What's wrong with Pa-Daddy?" she said. "He came flying up these stairs like his pants were on fire."

I didn't want to get into a family discussion in front of Ed Earl, so all I said was, "How should I know? Had a bad day, I guess."

Louise squinted her green cat's eyes at me. "You and Pa-Daddy have a fight?"

"No."

"Then what's going on between you two?"

With a mouthful of half-chewed peanuts, I managed to spit out, "None of your damn business."

"Quinnella Jeanne Ellerbee!" Louise was looking at me as if I'd just swallowed a whole wood rat right there in front of everybody and was sucking up the tail like some old piece of spaghetti.

"Well, it isn't," I said, trying to tone it down some. Truth is, I don't know what had got into me. It was like some crazy person was sitting up there inside my head, working my mouth controls. Seemed like every time I went to say something these days, it came out totally obnoxious.

Ed Earl was squirming around like he had poison ivy on his backside. I guess I'd made him pretty uncomfortable.

"I'd better find out what my dad wants," he said, getting to his feet. "I'll come back for the cypress knees later."

I just nodded, feeling too embarrassed to say much of anything else. Turned out I didn't have to, because suddenly we all heard a loud crack coming from somewhere down by the creek. If Ed Earl heard the shot, he didn't let on. He just kept heading toward the road and never looked back.

Louise jerked her chin in the direction of the sound. "Pa-Daddy. He barreled through the house, grabbed his hunting rifle, and headed out the door before you got here."

"So?" I shrugged. "Maybe we'll have something besides black-eyed peas and swamp cabbage to eat tonight."

Louise didn't even look at me. "I almost forgot. He said for you to come down when you got back." She popped open a peanut with her fingernail. Salty peanut water dribbled down the front of her T-shirt.

"Come down where?"

"To the creek, I guess."

"What for?"

"How should I know? Nobody ever tells me anything anymore."

I took a swallow of her iced tea. All that salty water was making me thirsty. "Well, maybe I don't feel like talking to him."

"I think you'd better. He seemed pretty upset."

I racked my brain trying to think of what I could have done wrong, but nothing came to mind.

Louise put her hand on my arm. "Please, Quinn. He won't talk to me. I'm worried about him. He's been acting kind of strange lately."

Well, I'd just sent a postcard to Mom trying to get some answers on that one, myself. So I guess I could understand Louise being upset. "What do you expect *me* to do about it?" I said. Because *I* sure didn't have any of those answers.

"Maybe you can get him to talk to you," Louise said, her voice half pleading. "You two were always good buddies."

I didn't feel like explaining to Louise that Pa-Daddy and I were barely on speaking terms, and as for good buddies—those days were long gone. But then it hit me, maybe Pa-Daddy was feeling bad about not standing up for me in front of Mrs. Taylor. Maybe he wanted to see me so he could apologize. So I finally agreed to find out what was going on.

I heard another shot just as I reached the creek. Then came the cracking sound of a branch and the dull thud when it hit the ground. I figured Pa-Daddy was probably just letting off a little steam.

I found him sitting on the bank with his back against a tree, the rifle by his side. He was staring up at a big old pine across the way. I could see where he had shot off the dead branch. "Nice shooting," I told him.

"I was aiming for the one above it," he said without even looking at me.

"Oh." I saw he had the lid off the cooler we keep down by the stream and was having himself a beer, so I helped myself to a can of RC Cola. We sat there, not saying anything, just sipping our drinks, till I couldn't take the quiet anymore. "Louise said you wanted to talk to me."

Pa-Daddy turned to look at me for the first time since I'd got there. Then he smiled and pointed to the creek. "I wonder if it's got a name."

"I don't think so," I told him. "Everybody just calls it the creek."

"Let's give it a name," he said. "We'll call it Comfort Creek, just like in Nanny Jo's stories."

I didn't know what to think about that. I mean, Pa-Daddy had grown up with those same stories. So I guess he could name the creek that if he wanted. The thing is, I kind of liked keeping Comfort Creek a made-up place, a place I could go in my imagination, even if Nanny Jo did keep insisting it was real. So I just said, "Is that what you wanted to talk to me about? Naming the creek?"

He rested his hand on the rifle and stroked it a few times like it was a pet dog. "Got a notice from the bank yesterday, saying our first mortgage payment was a week overdue." He shook his head like he couldn't quite believe it. "Can you beat that! A week. One week late, and already they're hounding me."

"So is that where you were this morning? You went to the bank to pay it?"

He nodded. "The bad news is I can't pay it." He took another sip of beer without looking at me. "We didn't get our final paychecks from the company yet. Something is holding them up."

I was trying real hard to keep my breathing even. Why was he telling me this? Why didn't he just take his bad news someplace else? "Maybe they don't have any money to pay you with," I suggested. "You said they were bankrupt."

Pa-Daddy looked about ready to cry, and I knew right then, just as he knew, that no money was going to be coming from the company. I'd never seen him so low. "I kept meaning to put a little of my paycheck away each week for emergencies, you know. But it seemed like we never had anything left over."

"What did the folks at the bank say?" I was trying hard to be practical and levelheaded, like I knew Mom would have been. "Did you explain it to them?"

"They don't want to hear no more hard-luck stories. Heard enough already this week, I suppose, considering all the folks been laid off by the company." Pa-Daddy took up his rifle again. I figured he'd spotted another dead limb. He fired off a shot, and another branch hit the dirt. "I thought I could work out something with the bank, smaller payments maybe, which is why I went over there this morning. They said I could just pay the interest if I wanted to, only since it's a new mortgage, the interest about takes up the whole payment."

I didn't understand half of what Pa-Daddy was telling me. But one thing had me worried. "Can the bank take our house?" A part of me was scared to death of the answer, but I had to know.

" 'Fraid so. But I'm still hoping I can work something out."

"You'll get a job," I said, trying to sound real positive. "Hey, maybe you could get a job pruning trees." I pointed to the branch he had just shot off.

Pa-Daddy laughed at that and shook his head. At least he hadn't lost his sense of humor. "I'm gonna try my best, darlin', but it don't look promising. I been to the unemployment agency. They say there's nothing out there for me. They say I ain't got nothing to offer. No skills, no high-school diploma, nothing."

"Well, then, why don't you get your diploma," I said, trying to be helpful.

Pa-Daddy gulped down the last of his beer. "I'm too old for that," he said. "I'd feel real out of place sitting in a classroom full of kids."

I guess he could tell I was feeling pretty disappointed in him. So he tried to look more cheerful. "I'm hoping that company from up in Hamilton County will start mining phosphate in the Pines," he said. "It'll mean work for a lot of folks."

"What about Nanny Jo and E.B.? Will they have to move?"

"Nanny Jo and E.B. live outside the Pines." He started scanning the woods for more dead branches, so I figured he didn't much want to talk about it anymore. But then he put down his gun like he had just thought of something.

"You know, Quinn, about the only thing we can count on in this world is change." He pointed to the creek. "There ain't no holding back change, any more'n you can keep that water there from going where it's headed." He looked over at me, I guess to see if I was getting his meaning. "Sometimes change works out better for some folks than others. Right now it ain't working in my favor."

"Maybe you can change along with it. You don't have to work in the mines. There's other work out there. You just have to learn new stuff first."

Pa-Daddy laughed right out loud at that. "Quinn honey, there's just some things we ain't got no control over. Things are gonna turn out the way they're meant to."

I got up to leave, because I didn't want to get into another argument with Pa-Daddy. These days, talking to him always left me feeling like I could go to bed and sleep for a week.

I wanted to scream, *Why you telling me all this? These are grown-up problems. Parents aren't supposed to be worrying their kids to death over stuff like this. What kind of dad are you!* But all I said was, "Is this what you wanted to talk to me about? This bank business?" It didn't look much like he'd been planning to apologize to me at all. It looked more like he just needed to unburden himself to somebody. So why did he have to pick me, considering the recent bad feelings between us? Why not Louise?

Pa-Daddy tilted his head and narrowed his eyes at me like he wasn't sure what I had on my mind, which was just as well. "I thought maybe you could help me break the news to Louise and Rhonda Fay this time. You're better at these things than me."

I didn't know what to say to that. I mean, the way I figured it, he'd brought me down here to get me to do his dirty work. It was downright cowardly. I closed my eyes to keep the tears from coming and stood up to leave. Pa-Daddy popped open another can of beer. I just stood there staring down at the water, because I couldn't look at him right then. As far as I was concerned, that old creek could just stay nameless. Because no matter what Pa-Daddy thought, I would never ever think of this place as Comfort Creek.

10

Shouting Folks

Well, I guess you could say Pa-Daddy's latest news about the bank wasn't exactly a big hit. We were already getting pretty tired of rabbit and mustard greens. And it was too late in the season to plant a vegetable garden. We all knew there weren't going to be any new school clothes this year, so nobody even bothered to ask.

Rhonda Fay had taken to going around barefoot so she could keep her sneakers all nice and new-looking for when school started in a few weeks. Louise took to calling her Saint Rhonda the Sneaker Martyr, seeing as how she was so dedicated to protecting those dumb shoes. In fact it was downright pitiful watching Rhonda Fay lifting herself up on her toes to pick her way across the meadow, trying not to get her bare feet too dirty or step on anything that wiggled.

Louise didn't say anything one way or the other about this latest development. But when Louise gets quiet about something, you can bet she's plotting. I knew I was right when I found Pa-Daddy's old road atlas under her bed. I figured she'd finally decided three more years was just too long to be living under such tormenting conditions.

Meantime, her boyfriend, Lloyd, had gotten his driver's license, so he and his friend Jim came to take Louise riding almost every day. Each time they tore down the driveway, raising all kinds of dust, I told myself not to expect to see Louise again. But then they always brought her back. At least they have so far.

The thing I noticed, though, was that Louise never invited Lloyd and Jim inside the house. She was always waiting for them on the front porch when they pulled up. Then she'd hop right in the car and never look back. Since Lloyd used to hang out at our house all the time in Panther Ridge, it wasn't like he'd never been inside before. So I finally figured out Louise didn't want him to know how we were living, without electricity and plumbing and all. Like he couldn't figure that out for himself? Anybody with half a brain could see there weren't any utility poles nearby, or any power lines running to the house. Still, old Lloyd wasn't the brightest person in the world, so maybe Louise did have him fooled.

On the days I wasn't working with Ed Earl, I spent my time planning my newspaper. Designing the layout, which means how many columns I wanted on each page, how I wanted the name of the paper to look, and that kind of stuff. My name, Quinnella Jeanne Ellerbee, would appear three times on the masthead, which was just fine with me. The masthead is what newspaper folks call the section that tells who the publisher and editor and all the other important people on the newspaper are. I even had a name for my newspaper, *The Comfort Creek Chronicle*. But *my* stories would be real stories about real people.

Me and Ed Earl spent the next three weeks making as many lamps as we could because school would be starting soon—which I was trying my hardest not to think about—and there wouldn't be much time for lamp making after that. By the end of August, we had ourselves almost four dozen lamps. Ed Earl called it our inventory. He said the selling season didn't really start till January, but we could set up a table at a couple of local craft shows in the meantime. I was kind of looking forward to it.

I'd already made over a hundred dollars helping with the business, doing the varnishing and cypress-knee hunting. Well, not actually a hundred dollars in money. Ed Earl was paying me in lamps. We figured out that seven of those lamps were mine to sell, since they cost fifteen dol-

lars each to make. If I sold them all at fifty dollars, I'd
make myself a couple hundred dollars' profit. I got a tingly
kind of excited whenever I thought about all that money,
which I did a lot.

But Ed Earl explained that I was supposed to put the
money right back into buying more supplies to make more
lamps, because that's how you build inventory, which is
how you build a business. He was right, of course, but
what he didn't know was that I planned on using the
money to start a different business. Once I had my computer, I wouldn't need lamp inventory. I'd just need customers. Folks to buy my newspaper.

Then one afternoon when I was coming home from Ed
Earl's, I spotted E.B.'s pickup in our front yard, wedged in
with a lot of other trucks and cars. A powerful lot of angry
shouting was coming from our house.

When I came through the front door, I found Nanny Jo
Pearl standing in the middle of our living room yelling up
a storm. She was holding on to her old black patent-
leather pocketbook, and anybody who tried to cross her
got that old purse stuck right in his face. That wispy bird-
feather hair of hers was floating in all directions like it
couldn't lie still for a minute with all that ruckus going on.

"Nobody, I mean nobody, is gonna make me and E.B.
move. Y'all hear? Nobody!" She swung around and
stabbed her purse in Pa-Daddy's direction. "And you,

112

sonny, you're gonna have to make up your mind just whose side you're on."

I inched my way across the room to the kitchen door, where Louise was standing. She was probably thinking the same thing I was, that she could make a quick getaway out the back door if she had to. The whole room was filled with angry folks. Kinfolks, folks who had worked with Pa-Daddy at the Panther Ridge mine, folks everywhere, like fleas on a dog. And all of them yelling at once.

Pa-Daddy was sitting on the sofa. He seemed to be doing a fine job of inspecting his boots right then. That's when E.B. went over and sat down next to him. "Nanny Jo's a mite overwrought today, Claude." He patted Pa-Daddy on the shoulder with his wrinkly old hand. "Truth is, this news about the mining company trying to buy us all out has got a lot of folks pretty upset."

I spotted Rhonda Fay sitting behind us at the kitchen table. I guess for once she didn't much want to be the center of attention. She had her elbows on the table and her hands over her ears, sitting real still, staring down at a bowlful of boiled peanuts. But she wasn't eating any. I stepped back and grabbed a handful.

"These are mine," she snapped. "Get your own."

"You aren't eating them anyway." I could tell she was going to give me a fight. "Hush up," I told her before she had a chance to say anything. "I want to hear what's going on."

"Bunch of crazy folks," she muttered. "Everybody yell-

113

ing and screeching. Worse than some old henhouse with a fox loose in it."

"Hush up," I said again, reaching for a few more peanuts. But Rhonda Fay snapped her fingers around my wrist and twisted it like she was wringing an old wet dishcloth.

I managed to snatch up a few more nuts with my free hand, then took up my post at the kitchen door. I didn't want to miss anything.

Louise was leaning against the doorjamb with her arms folded, watching Nanny Jo swing that pocketbook every which way. You would have thought Nanny Jo was fending off a whole street gang all by herself.

"You don't have to sell to nobody," Pa-Daddy explained to Nanny Jo. "Besides, I don't think they're planning to mine your area. Just a section of the Pines."

"They want to mine all the area around the Pines, too, Claude Ellerbee. They want to mine Ellerbee land. Land that's been in our family for generations." Nanny Jo stood over him with her purse stuck under her arm and her arms folded in front of her. "Don't you pay attention, boy?"

"But you don't have to sell to them," Pa-Daddy reminded her.

"Don't be a fool. Remember what happened to Ike Spivey?" Nanny Jo circled the room, collecting nods from all the kinfolk. We all knew what had happened to Ike Spivey. The phosphate company Pa-Daddy used to work for wanted to buy up Ike's farm. But he wouldn't sell. So

114

they up and bought all the land around him. Mined their way right up to his property line. Had him surrounded. Finally, all that mining destroyed his groundwater and he had to move. Naturally, nobody wanted to buy a farm with bad water, so he finally gave in and sold it to the mining company. But they only gave him one-tenth of what they had originally offered. Said the property wasn't worth a plugged nickel seeing as how the groundwater was all polluted.

Uncle Jeb leaned forward, his large belly flopping over his belt, and said, "Nanny Jo's right, Claude. They're going to get us one way or the other."

"Us?" Pa-Daddy narrowed his eyes at Uncle Jeb. "You run a Laundromat. They ain't going to bother with the likes of you."

"If folks sell their land and leave the area, where's my business going to come from? Tell me that, big brother."

Pa-Daddy heaved a sigh. I could see all these folks were beginning to wear him down.

Joe Whiggs, who had helped Pa-Daddy put in our manual pump, stood up, facing Nanny Jo. He was holding his Miami Dolphins cap in his hands, twisting it back and forth. Little beads of sweat had sprouted on his upper lip. "Excuse me, ma'am, with all due respect, hundreds of us is out of work since the Panther Ridge Company went belly up. We got families to feed."

"I got a family to feed, too," Pa-Daddy said. "I got to think about that first, Nanny Jo."

Nanny Jo spun around so fast I thought she'd tip over. "Family has got to stick together at a time like this, boy. Mining ain't everything. Now I know E.B.'s talked to you about managing them groves of ours, and the pay ain't nothing to scoff at, either." She glanced down at E.B. and for one tiny moment her face got sort of soft. "Besides, E.B. could use some help running the place. He ain't as young as he used to be."

E.B. took a minute to look respectfully indignant, but I could tell he was hoping Pa-Daddy would take Nanny Jo up on her offer. Poor old E.B. had to work pretty hard managing the local folks who did the spraying and the hoeing, and then organizing the migrant workers during picking time.

Rhonda Fay must have heard Nanny Jo's offer, because she had left her post at the kitchen table and was standing next to Louise. I guess we were all waiting to see what Pa-Daddy would say about going to work for Nanny Jo. But as soon as he started shaking his head, I knew he was thinking how Nanny Jo was trying to run his life again, and how she was probably just hiring him to keep him from siding with the mining folks.

Uncle Jeb stood up and squeezed his pudgy hands into his pockets. He looked down at Pa-Daddy, his upper lip curling up in a sneer. "Like Nanny Jo says, family's got to stick together at times like this. If you ain't with us, then you're against us. Which means you ain't family no more."

116

Not family anymore? I shot a panicky look at Pa-Daddy. He wouldn't risk splitting up the family, would he? My heart was pounding so loud I was sure everybody in the living room could hear it, especially since the room had got so quiet all of a sudden.

Pa-Daddy sat there in the middle of all that silence like he was hoping it would swallow him up, or even better, swallow up all the other folks in the room. Either way he didn't look too comfortable.

Just then there was a knock at the front door. Everyone shifted their eyes in that direction, like maybe they were expecting an angel from heaven to step in and straighten out this whole mess. But it was only Lloyd come to take Louise driving. He stood in the open doorway in his Led Zeppelin T-shirt, with his skinny shoulders hunched forward and his hands stuffed in the pockets of his ratty old jeans, surveying all the folks; then he took a step back out onto the porch.

Louise bolted across the room. "Sorry, I gotta go," she said. "Lloyd's here."

Nanny Jo narrowed her dark bird eyes. "Who's this Floyd?"

"Lloyd," Louise mumbled at the floor.

"What?"

"My boyfriend."

Nanny Jo perked up at that. Meeting new boyfriends was always an occasion. "Well, bring him on in here." She waved her hand toward the door. "Come on in here, boy.

117

We ain't gonna eat you alive." The thing is, Nanny Jo had already met Lloyd at least ten times, except for some reason, she never seemed to remember him.

I could tell by the look on Louise's face that she didn't want Lloyd coming inside, but it was too late. Poor old Lloyd stepped through the door, looking like it was execution day, which wasn't all that far from the truth. Louise stepped up to him, and he put his arm around her waist like he might fall over if he couldn't lean on her right then. Louise's face was bright red and growing darker by the minute. I couldn't tell if it was from pure embarrassment, or if Lloyd was holding on too tight.

Most everybody there already knew Lloyd because his father owned the only gas station in the Pines area. So they all nodded, and a few shook hands, and then everybody settled down again. For the moment, at least, everybody had forgotten about the new mining company. Families are like that. One minute they're fighting like a pack of pit bulls, and the next minute they're putting up a great front for any stranger who might happen along. Even for Lloyd, who wasn't really a stranger, although he was pretty strange.

"Well, it's nice meeting you, boy," Nanny Jo said. "I know your daddy. He's a good man." Which is exactly what she said all those other times she got introduced to Lloyd. Then Nanny Jo set her patent-leather pocketbook on the floor by her chair, so I knew she'd declared a temporary truce. There would be no more feuding, not that day anyway.

As soon as Lloyd and Louise left the house, Nanny Jo stood up to go. I guess she figured enough was enough for one afternoon. Even though nobody actually said anything, I could tell everybody had decided to follow Nanny Jo's lead. But we all knew the truce wouldn't last.

Nanny Jo gave me a pinch on the cheek as she went through the front door. "Talk some sense into that daddy of yours, Quinny girl," she said.

I wanted to tell her there was just no talking to Pa-Daddy about anything these days, but I didn't. Besides, maybe she'd already figured it out for herself.

"Nanny Jo," I said, "any mail come to your house addressed to me?"

Nanny Jo cocked her head sideways like she was trying to remember. "Don't think so," she said. "You expecting a letter from somebody?"

"Nothing important," I said casually. "Just a letter from a friend I wrote to."

"Well, why'd you give your friend my address?" she asked, narrowing her eyes at me. "Why didn't you give her your own?"

I couldn't think of what to say to that, so I stood there looking downright stupid.

"You wrote to your mama, didn't you?" she said, lowering her voice to hardly a whisper.

What could I do? Like I said, Nanny Jo's got this second sight. So I just nodded. And then she nodded right back at me.

"Well, it'll be our secret," she said. And I knew she meant it.

11

Taking Sides

Two days later, school started. Ed Earl had already explained to me that our school wasn't very big. Nothing like the middle school I used to go to in Panther Ridge. So I wasn't expecting much. Things are less disappointing that way.

Truth is, though, I was pretty nervous. I felt like I was carrying around a twenty-pound sack of flour inside my chest. Course, I had bigger things to worry about than school. So far nobody from the bank had come to take our house away, but just because Pa-Daddy didn't talk about it anymore didn't mean it wasn't going to happen. I kept most of my favorite things in a cardboard box under my bed just in case the bank folks didn't give us time to pack up anything when they came.

School turned out to be one more big disappointment.

Even bigger than I'd prepared myself for. Ed Earl had told me it was small, but I figured each grade would at least have its own classroom. What this building looked like was a big flat letter H. It wasn't even made of brick. It was old clapboard painted—you aren't gonna believe this—baby blue! I wondered if the regional high school where Louise was going looked like this. Because if it did, she'd be pretty upset about it.

There were only five rooms in the whole building: two classrooms, a small library, the cafeteria, and an auditorium set smack in the middle like its job was to hold the whole building together. And there weren't but thirty-two kids in the whole school.

One classroom had grades one through four, the other had grades five through eight. At least I wasn't stuck in the same classroom with Rhonda Fay, her being in the fourth grade this year. Ed Earl, who is the same age as me, ended up a grade ahead of me on account of he had skipped a grade when he was younger, which didn't surprise me one little bit.

This school didn't look like the kind of place that would even have a newspaper I could be editor of. I guess that was the biggest disappointment of all. More than anything, I wanted to be back in my regular sixth-grade class with all my old friends, learning to be a newspaperwoman like I'd planned before all this moving business happened.

Besides, that first morning was just plain weird. It

started with our teacher, Ms. Fromberg, giving assignments to the different grades. While we were all working, she brought the fifth-graders, all five of them, up to her desk to work on math. Then she sent the fifth-graders back, and brought the seventh-graders up to her desk to work on grammar. Even though they kept their voices low, it was still hard to concentrate.

After school, me and Ed Earl headed for the bus.

"Isn't that your dad over there?" he said, pointing to the driveway next to the school.

"Where?" I looked to where he was pointing and, sure enough, there was Pa-Daddy waving for me to come on. Rhonda Fay was already in the front seat, looking pretty worried. I couldn't figure out what Pa-Daddy was doing there. My heart started skittering all over the place.

I tossed my book bag on the floor of the truck and climbed up next to Rhonda Fay. Nobody said anything, which was fine with me. Pa-Daddy just drove along, his hands gripping the steering wheel so tight his knuckles had turned yellow white. Even though I didn't have the faintest notion where we were headed, I wasn't about to ask him.

Finally, I guess Rhonda Fay couldn't stand the silence anymore. "What's going on?" she said to Pa-Daddy.

"Nanny Jo and E.B. was over to the house this morning." His voice sounded grim. "Things didn't go too good."

"Why not? What happened?" she said. I already knew what Pa-Daddy was going to say, even if Rhonda Fay didn't. I knew they had all been feuding again.

Pa-Daddy tugged at the brim of his engineer's hat, then ran the palms of his big hands back and forth around the steering wheel a few times. I could tell he was stalling. "I don't know, darlin'. Same stuff as the other day when all them folks was over to our house. All Nanny Jo talks about is me coming to work for them and helping to keep the mining company out. It's getting to be like listening to some old broken record."

His eyes were blinking a mile a minute like they always do when he's puzzling over something. "Well, I thanked them kindly for offering me a job. But I had to say no all the same." He reached up and pulled at his chin like he was tugging some old imaginary beard. "I wish they'd try to see my side of it. Mining's been my whole life. It's what I do best. I don't know nothing else. I got to fight for what I want, just like they got to fight for what they believe."

Rhonda Fay reached over and patted his arm. She can be a real brown-noser sometimes. "I know that, Pa-Daddy. And that's what Nanny Jo's doing, too. She's fighting to wear you down, so you'll be one less person siding with the mining company. You shouldn't take it personal."

"Oh no?" Pa-Daddy looked over at her and laughed. It wasn't a happy laugh. "Nanny Jo's talking about disowning me, which means my family, which means you, too."

"What? What does that mean, disown us?" Rhonda Fay looked alarmed. So was I, but I pretended like I wasn't even listening to their conversation.

Pa-Daddy's eyes started blinking again. "It means she won't want to have nothing to do with us. She won't consider us family no more."

I couldn't imagine my life without Nanny Jo or E.B. in it, or without Sunday barbecues at their house with all the family. And deep down, I knew Nanny Jo couldn't imagine it, either. "She doesn't mean it," I told Pa-Daddy. "She's just trying to get you to see things her way."

"Which is what she's been doing my whole life," Pa-Daddy snapped back. "Well, it's time we straightened this mess out once and for all." Pa-Daddy slid a sheepish look our way. "That's why I picked you two up at school today. I figured if anybody could make things right with Nanny Jo, it was you."

"Sure, Pa-Daddy," Rhonda Fay chimed in. "We'll help."

I wanted to shout, *Speak for yourself, Rhonda Fay!* But I didn't. I didn't say much of anything after that, seeing as how I suddenly noticed Pa-Daddy was making me do his dirty work again, wanting me to get him out of a mess he'd gone and got himself into. But there was something else. I was beginning to wonder how much of his stubbornness was about wanting to work for the new mine, and how much was about spiting Nanny Jo. It was getting pretty confusing. And, personally, I didn't want to find myself smack in the middle of somebody else's feud. Besides, Nanny Jo Pearl is about the stubbornest woman I know. Did Pa-Daddy really think me and Rhonda Fay could get her to change her mind?

But that wasn't the worst part. The worst part was, I wasn't even on Pa-Daddy's side. I didn't want the new mining company buying up the Pines and all the land around it. I didn't want my friends to have to move, or Nanny Jo to give up her house and the groves, and I sure as heck didn't want to be disowned, even though I didn't believe for a minute Nanny Jo would really do it.

It turned out Nanny Jo wasn't even home when we finally got there. E.B.'s truck was parked out front, but Nanny Jo's old green Nova was nowhere in sight. Usually E.B. drives her most places in the pickup, but today it looked like she'd taken off on her own.

Pa-Daddy knocked on the front door for a while, then headed around back. Nanny Jo never bothers to lock the back door. Rhonda Fay and I followed him and stood by while he stepped inside the kitchen and yelled, "Anybody home?" But nobody answered.

"It's not like E.B. and Nanny Jo to take the Nova," Pa-Daddy said, blinking his puzzlement.

"Maybe E.B.'s still here," Rhonda Fay suggested, which turned out to be right, because just then we heard a noisy pop, sort of like a little explosion, followed by the sound of glass shattering and a loud "Damn" coming from the smokehouse. We all looked at each other in surprise, then took off in the direction of the noise.

Pa-Daddy and Rhonda Fay got there first. I poked my head between them and peeked in the door. There sat old E.B. right on the dirt floor, with about five empty bottles around him.

"Howdy," he said, grinning so we could see the dark spaces where some of his teeth used to be. "Come on in and set a spell."

We all stepped inside but nobody sat down.

"Just lost another one." E.B. pointed to a large barrel with an old croaker sack thrown over the top. "Guess I capped them too soon." He took a swallow from the bottle in his hand, then tipped his head in the direction of the barrel. "Help yourself, Claude. I'm gonna lose 'em all anyway."

He looked over at Rhonda Fay and me. "Soda in the fridge, little ladies."

I sat down beside him. "No thanks."

"This some of your home brew?" Pa-Daddy said, reaching inside the barrel for a bottle. E.B. sometimes brews his own beer. But he hasn't done it for a long time, seeing as how Nanny Jo's the disapproving type.

"Yes sir. My very own recipe," E.B. told Pa-Daddy. He looked real down about it, though. "You'd have thought after all these years I'd know how to time the capping." He shook his head, and the sunlight coming through the door glinted off his thick glasses, hiding his eyes for a minute. "I must be losing my touch." He took a deep swallow from the bottle in his hand. "Can't bear to see it go to waste, so I'm enjoying as much of it as I can."

Pa–Daddy was staring down inside the barrel. "Looks like a lot of broken glass in here, E.B."

"Should still be a few good ones left."

Pa–Daddy took the bottle opener that hung from the doorknob on a string, opened a bottle, then sat down across from E.B., bracing himself against the smokehouse wall. "When's Nanny Jo getting back?" he asked.

E.B. got this worried look on his face, like he had forgot all about Nanny Jo. "Not too soon, I hope," he said. "She ain't gonna like this one bit."

"Where's she gone?" I asked him.

"Over to Mayville. Something about setting up a craft fair and flea market so's they can make money to hire a lawyer for the Pines folks."

Mayville is the nearest big town to the Pines. Course *big* in our county means there's a real streetlight in the center of town. The Pines isn't really a town. It's a place. A place where a lot of folks decided they wanted to build their houses. But there aren't any stores or anything.

Well, Pa–Daddy sort of pulled into himself like he had heard the sound of a rattlesnake in the distance. "Hiring a lawyer? What for?"

Before E.B. got to answer, old Rhonda Fay jumped

right in. "Nanny Jo's going to have a table at a craft fair? No kidding? What's she going to sell?" Rhonda Fay's real big on county fairs and flea markets. She likes going anyplace where there's stuff to buy.

E.B. rubbed his thumb and forefinger along the bridge of his nose, pondering on this a minute. "Quilts, I think."

I snuck a look at Pa-Daddy. His whole body looked like it had froze solid.

"New ones or old ones?" I asked E.B. I know the answer wouldn't mean much to anybody else, but it did to me. Some of Nanny Jo's old quilts had belonged to her mama and her grandma. They've been in the family for as long as any of us could remember. She always promised that someday they would be ours—mine, Rhonda Fay's, and Louise's—on account of them being part of our family history.

E.B. took a swallow of his beer like he was giving my question real serious thought. "Both," he said finally. "Yes, I believe that's what she said. She was selling them all if it'd help."

My stomach got real cold, like I'd downed a gallon of ice cream in one swallow. I felt real bad, but I could understand why Nanny Jo was doing it. Truth is, I knew I wanted to help, too. If Nanny Jo was willing to do something that drastic, then this whole thing was pretty important to her. If she and the Pines folks were going to put up a fight, I wanted to be in on it.

129

Pa-Daddy still hadn't said a word. He just sipped at his beer and listened. Finally he said, "What craft fair is this y'all talking about?"

"The one the Pines folks is organizing," E.B. told him, as if he hadn't already explained that. "They want to hire a lawyer to keep that new mining company out."

"Well," Pa-Daddy said, "if them folks think bringing in some slick city lawyer is gonna save them, they're in for one mighty big rude awakening."

E.B. slid his back up against the wall and got himself to his feet, but I had the feeling it wouldn't be for long, because he kept swaying back and forth. Finally he grabbed hold of the top of the barrel to steady himself.

"Remember whose land you're sitting on, boy," he said to Pa-Daddy. "And whose beer you're drinking." His glasses started to slide down his nose, and he poked them back up with his finger, like he wanted to make sure Pa-Daddy got his point. "Now you might think your Nanny Jo is being a mite stubborn on this one, but I happen to support her all the way. I thought you come over here to make up, but now it don't look that way to me. So maybe you folks should be heading on home."

Pa-Daddy set the half-finished beer on the ground beside him and got to his feet. "Fine with me," he said, grabbing the front of his engineer's hat and setting it firmer on his head.

All I know is, as we were walking back to the pickup, I kept looking around Nanny Jo's place, trying to take it all in, packing it away someplace in my mind, and wondering if we would ever set foot on it again.

12

Joining the Cause

I spent the next few days thinking a lot about what would happen if that new mining company took over the Pines and all the land around it, and I knew in my heart what I had to do. I'd seen what strip mining had done to the place where Pa-Daddy used to work. Water got polluted. Wildlife got wiped out. Houses got tore down. And this time it would be the houses of friends and family. Some things were just worth fighting for, even if Pa-Daddy saw it different.

Meanwhile, things were going from bad to worse, as they say. The bank was sending letters to Pa-Daddy almost every couple of days. Every time I heard a knock at the door, I was sure somebody was coming to tell us we had to move on.

Then Pa-Daddy got this job over in Bridgetown, helping to dig ditches for a new sewer line, and we all breathed a little easier. That is, until we found out the job was only going to last for a couple of weeks.

"At least he's trying," Louise said.

It was the first Saturday after school had started, and me and Louise and Rhonda Fay were all sitting around the kitchen table. Pa-Daddy was out digging ditches, so I had decided to call a family meeting, which is what my mom used to do whenever there was a family crisis. And this whole mining-company business sure counted as a crisis, to my way of thinking.

Louise was busy painting her fingernails with that gross purple stuff she wears, on account of Lloyd was coming over later. Rhonda Fay kept nagging her to let her try some. Rhonda Fay's darn good at nagging. In fact, if they gave out awards for that kind of thing, I expect she'd have a whole wall full of blue ribbons by now. So I knew Louise would finally give in, even though she only had a little bit left in the bottle, and no money to buy any more. It was just easier that way.

"Maybe Pa-Daddy's digging job'll become permanent," Rhonda Fay said, pulling the nail polish over to her side of the table.

"Maybe, maybe not," Louise said. "But we can't just sit by and let the bank take our house."

"Yes we can," Rhonda Fay said.

That really got a rise out of Louise, which surprised me since about the only thing that got her attention anymore was Lloyd. It was like she didn't even know the rest of us existed. "Rhonda Fay!" she snapped.

"What?"

Louise let out a little snort. "How can you say such a thing?"

"Easy." Rhonda Fay jutted that pointy chin of hers right in Louise's direction. "They can have this old Swamp House. I hate it." And she went right back to painting her nails.

Now, the truth is, even though I hated living in the swamp, and even though my plan had to do with us getting out of there, I felt this little tug in my chest. After all, I've spent my whole life in this house. And even if it isn't much of a house, it's still the only one we got. Besides, I had lots of good memories from when we lived in Panther Ridge, memories of Mom and stuff. Still, I had to agree with Rhonda Fay. Even if it meant letting the bank take our home. "We've got to come up with a plan," I said.

"What kind of plan?" Louise asked.

"I don't know," I said, although I really did know because I'd been thinking about it for days. "Maybe we could have a table at the fair." I'd been planning to write Nanny Jo and ask if she wanted me to help her and E.B. with their table at the fair, but then it had come to me—I could have my own table. I could sell the cypress lamps. I knew it meant giving up my computer money. But if Nanny Jo could sell the family quilts, I could sure do without a computer for a while longer.

"How's that gonna help?" Louise asked. "I thought all the money was supposed to go to hiring a lawyer for the Pines folks."

"Exactly," I said.

Louise was blowing on her fingernails to dry them. I could see she was thinking, because her eyebrows got all puckered. "You got everything all backward," she said finally. "If we help the Pines folks fight that mining company, then Pa-Daddy'll never get work, and the bank is sure to take our house."

Which is just what I had in mind, although I didn't say so right up front. I'd planned it all out so that the bank would take this old Swamp House. Then we'd all have to move to Nanny Jo's, because it would be the only place left for us to go. I figured Pa-Daddy could manage the groves, I could go to my old school, and we'd all have electricity and plumbing again. So that's how I explained it to Louise and Rhonda Fay.

Rhonda Fay was especially enthusiastic. She took to dancing around the kitchen, singing, "No more outhouse" over and over.

"Better contain yourself, Rhonda Fay," Louise said in this real heavy voice. "You'll mess up your nail polish." But even that didn't stop old Rhonda Fay, who'd about

135

twirled herself silly by then. "I can't believe you two would do something so sneaky behind Pa-Daddy's back," Louise said, barely able to sputter out the words.

"Some things are more important," I told her. "Nanny Jo could lose the groves if this company comes in. That land's been in our family for generations. It's our heritage." Now, the thing is, I hadn't planned on saying any of that stuff. It just sort of popped out. And when it did, I knew that was how I really felt. The bank could take the Swamp House, for all I cared. But the groves and Nanny Jo's, that was something else.

Louise was eyeing me suspiciously, like she knew I was up to something. "This is Ellerbee land, too," she reminded us. "Pa-Daddy's fighting as hard for this place as Nanny Jo is for hers."

I didn't know what to say to that, so I just yelled out, "If Mom was here, she'd have moved us to Nanny Jo's long ago!" Which didn't have anything to do with what Louise had just said, but it was all I could think of. "She wouldn't make us live like this."

"You shouldn't be talking about Mom," Louise reminded me. Her nostrils were flaring, so I could tell she was getting angry.

"Why not? Because Pa-Daddy said so?" I was getting pretty upset, myself. "He's the one who got us into all this." I wanted to shout right in her face that I'd gone and broken another of Pa-Daddy's stupid rules. That I'd written to Mom. But since she hadn't written back yet, I de-

136

cided to keep my mouth shut. Why go and get *their* hopes up, too? Especially if Mom never wrote back.

Louise went over to the pump for a glass of water. I could tell she was trying to calm herself down. Sweat was dribbling down the sides of her face. She looked kind of tired, like some old wilted sunflower. "You ain't being fair to him," she said finally. "He's been through a lot, with the divorce, and losing his job, and all." She stood there rubbing the cool glass back and forth across her forehead.

"Well, he ain't exactly been fair to us, either," Rhonda Fay chimed in. "I vote we help Nanny Jo and the Pines folks."

Louise just shook her head, but before she could say anything, Lloyd showed up at the back door, which put an end to our meeting. It made me mad, him showing up right then. We still had a lot of stuff to settle. But the Ellerbees never discuss family business in front of folks who aren't family.

I expected Louise to just walk on out of the house like she always does and take off with Lloyd in his old Toyota pickup. But instead, she just signaled him to come on in. Now that really surprised me. But I guess she wasn't thinking clear, with all this family stuff on her mind.

Lloyd sat down across from me, and the first thing I noticed was he'd got this new nose ring. We'd all thought he'd about gone the limit the time he tried to bleach his hair and it turned out bright orange. For weeks me and Rhonda Fay went around calling him Ronald McDonald, which really made Louise mad. But this nose ring was something else.

I leaned way over till I was only a few inches from Lloyd's face. "Hey Louise," I said, "now you can really lead Lloyd around by the nose. All you gotta do is hook up a rope to that ring there, and you can pull him around like an old cow."

Lloyd's face turned the color of a nasty bruise. He shot a look at Louise, like he was silently asking her permission to kill me on the spot. Louise grabbed me by the upper arm and yanked me right out of my chair. But I wasn't about to let it go. It was just too good. "You didn't need a nose ring for that," I told him. "Louise here's been doing just fine without one. Should've saved your money."

Louise twisted my arm so bad I thought it'd pop right out of its socket. "Get out of here!" she shrieked at the top of her lungs. "Both of you. Just get out of this house. *Now!*"

"It's our house, too," Rhonda Fay reminded her. And she wrapped her ankles around the chair legs, so I knew she wasn't going to budge. Stubbornness runs deep in our family.

So in the end, Lloyd and Louise took off in his pickup, which is what me and Rhonda Fay knew was going to happen anyway. But the part that made me feel really bad was that I knew Louise had taken up sides with Pa-Daddy, which meant me and Rhonda Fay were on our own. And we didn't know the first thing about running a table at a craft fair. I needed somebody to help me who had experience, and right off I knew that person was Ed Earl. All I had to do was talk him into joining the cause.

Two days later, me and Rhonda Fay cornered Ed Earl in the back of the school bus. "I think I found us a good craft fair for the lamps," I said, sitting down next to him. Rhonda Fay sat in a seat across the aisle from us.

"Yeah, where?" He bent over to inspect his sneaker, which was making funny little sucking sounds. But even though he didn't look up, I could tell I'd got his attention.

"In Mayville. Some folks down in the Pines are organizing it. E.B. told us about it."

"Yuck!" he said, lifting his shoe. A Popsicle wrapper was stuck to the bottom. "Chocolate," he announced. "It's melted all over the floor." The rule is, we're not supposed to have food on the bus, but nobody ever pays any attention to it.

"Are you listening to me?" I said.

He peeled that sticky old paper off his shoe and let it plop back on the floor. "Do I have a choice?"

I just ignored that. "It's going to be a big craft fair and flea market. They're trying to raise money to hire a lawyer to keep that new mining company out."

"How big?" he asked.

"Big. Very big," I told him, although the truth was, I didn't have a clue. It's just that I wanted to get him as excited about the fair as I was.

"Do you think they would let us set up a table?" he asked. He was beginning to sound a little bit interested.

"Maybe. I could try to find out." My heart was racing as fast as a horse outrunning a lightning bolt. It was going to happen. We were going to pull it off.

"It sounds like a pretty big craft fair. We could probably sell a lot of lamps," he said.

"Everybody's donating all the money they make to hire a lawyer to keep that new mining company out of the Pines," Rhonda Fay volunteered, leaning across the aisle.

"Hold it, hold it," Ed Earl said. "What's this about donating *all* the proceeds?"

I shot Rhonda Fay a dirty look. She just never knew when to keep her mouth shut. "Well," I said to Ed Earl, "if the folks are trying to raise money to hire a lawyer, I don't think they'd let people sell things who weren't there for the cause. It would be misleading the people who bought stuff thinking they were helping. Wouldn't it?" I really wasn't all that sure how it worked myself, but what I said to Ed Earl sounded about right to me.

"Maybe I don't want to do this after all," he said.

My heart suddenly felt like it'd dropped into my belly. "Well, I can still donate my seven lamps, can't I? I worked for them. They're mine, right?"

Ed Earl looked thoroughly disgusted with me. "They're yours," he said. "It's fine with me if you want to throw away all your profits, but don't expect me to do it."

"It's really for a good cause. You'd be giving a lot of folks a fighting chance to keep their land." I could see I wasn't getting through to him, so I switched tactics. "And what about all the wildlife?" I added. "You want them to get mined under? You think they can adapt fast enough to dodge those big drag lines while they tear up the land?" Drag lines are these excavating cranes that move all the topsoil away and then dig out the phosphate. Not much is left when they get through. Just big piles of dirt and lots of holes. "And what about those high-pressure water guns? I sure hope no little critters get in the way of those guns."

Ed Earl is real big on preserving endangered animals and stuff. He talked a lot about it while we worked on our lamps. Endangered critters are just about Ed Earl's favorite subject. He even told me once that he was planning to be a zoologist someday.

Ed Earl started twisting his hair around his finger. I could tell I had him worried. "I guess I could donate a few lamps," he said finally. "I'd sure hate to see the land stripped like that."

I patted him on the shoulder. "That's the spirit," I said, just as the bus pulled up in front of the school. Now all I had to do was make sure Pa-Daddy and Louise didn't find out what we were up to.

13

The Craft Fair and Flea Market

The day of the craft fair and flea market turned out to be just about the sunniest Saturday anybody'd want. But even though it was the third week in September, I knew by noon it would feel like we were all breathing under water.

Ed Earl's dad drove us to Mayville that morning. Rhonda Fay had come along too, and the four of us were squooshed together in the front of the Murdochs' pickup. In the back of the truck we had a long fold-up table and twelve cypress-knee lamps. I was going to donate the money from the sale of all seven of my lamps. Giving up my computer money and all those dreams about having my own newspaper was probably one of the hardest things I'd ever faced. But I knew I was doing the right thing.

Ed Earl had decided to donate five of his lamps. He told me he couldn't donate all of them because then he would be out of business. He wouldn't have any inventory left, which meant no "projected income" to buy more supplies to make more lamps.

Two months ago I wouldn't have known what "projected income" even meant. But I'd learned a lot about running a business since I'd gone to work for Ed Earl. He's a pretty good teacher. I was going to miss him when he and his folks moved back to the university town in December.

Pa-Daddy and Louise thought I'd gone over to Ed Earl's that morning like I always did. I told them Rhonda Fay was coming with me to help out. Naturally I couldn't tell them we had a table at the craft fair. It pained me, lying like that, but I think it would have hurt them a whole lot more if they'd known I was helping Nanny Jo and the Pines folks. Louise hadn't said another word about our family meeting, so we figured she'd forgotten all about our plan. Rhonda Fay and me made a pact not to tell her we were going through with it, seeing as how she had been getting pretty soft about Pa-Daddy, telling us we should try to be more understanding and all. Frankly, we just didn't trust her anymore. As far as we were concerned, she had gone over to the enemy.

Mayville looked all dressed up for a party that morning. Folks had hung bright red, white, and blue streamers overhead, draped from one side of the street to the other. Red, white, and blue balloons danced from around telephone poles, signposts, the doorknobs of shop doors, just about

143

everywhere you looked. It seemed from the colors they picked, the committee wanted folks to be reminded they lived in a democracy, which meant the voices of the people counted for something. And they were all planning to raise their voices pretty loud before this whole mining business was over. I was glad the committee had agreed to let us be a part of it, telling us it was okay to sell our lamps and all. Ed Earl had made all the arrangements on account of we didn't want my family to find out.

Mr. Murdoch helped me and Ed Earl set up our table in the section of Main Street that had been set aside for the craft fair. Another section, further down, was for the flea-market tables. There was even a section with food stands and picnic tables. Everywhere you looked, folks were setting up tables and spreading out their goods.

I spotted Mary Alice Taylor and her mom. They were arranging a lot of stuffed bears made out of old quilting pieces on a card table they had brought. Mary Alice had that mile-long hair of hers wove together in one fat French braid.

I nudged Rhonda Fay and I said, loud as could be, "They call those old things *crafts*?" I waved my hand like those bears were pesky flies I was trying to shoo away. "Somebody ought to tell them they belong over in the flea-market section." Mary Alice just rolled her eyes in disgust and looked the other way.

Rhonda Fay let out a little snort of agreement, but she still waved to Mrs. Taylor and Mary Alice. She can be pretty two-faced sometimes. Anyway, they didn't wave back. I guess there were still some hard feelings about the "haircutting incident."

Even Tanner McPherson was at the fair. His folks had a table on the flea-market side. Only, at that moment, he came wandering up to Mary Alice's table and started to help her unpack the bears. Mary Alice slanted her eyes my way and gave me a sly grin, making sure I noticed. I tried to pretend like I hadn't, but the truth is, I wanted to smack her. After all, Tanner's had a crush on me since the first grade. And even if I wasn't sweet on him, it still seemed kind of strange, him hanging around another girl. And not just any girl—slimy old Mary Alice. Besides, I could swear I saw her mouth the words *Swamp Thing*.

But then I noticed Tanner was frowning at Ed Earl, and I could tell by the worried look on his face that he was wondering who Ed Earl was and what I was doing there with him. So maybe Mary Alice thought Tanner was helping her out because he liked her. But I figured, knowing Tanner, he was doing it to get my attention. Which, I have to admit, he did.

The thing is, he did look kind of cute in those new baggy cutoffs he was wearing. He had his baseball cap turned around backward, and a clump of his hair was sticking out through the open space above the band. I don't know what got into me all of a sudden, but there I was, smiling and giving him a big wave like I was real pleased to see him, which I guess I was.

145

"I'm gonna look around some," Rhonda Fay said, bursting into my thoughts. She was eyeing me and Tanner suspiciously. I mean, I guess she figured Mary Alice wasn't any competition at all, and since I'd never given Tanner much notice, maybe she thought she had a chance with him. But there I was, flirting with Tanner like my life depended on it, which was the last thing she wanted to see.

"Just don't forget we're here to sell stuff, not buy it," I shouted after her as she started to wander off. But I could tell she wasn't paying me any mind.

Mr. Murdoch helped us unpack the last of the lamps and set them on the table. "Well, if you kids don't need me anymore, I think I'll head back to the house. I have to get these latest chapters of my book to my editor by the end of next week."

"That's okay, Dad," Ed Earl said. "We can handle it from here on."

Mr. Murdoch glanced down at his watch. "It's almost eight o'clock. What time do you want me to pick you up?"

Ed Earl looked over at me. I had no idea when the fair was supposed to be over. "I guess things will be closing down around dinnertime," I told him.

"Well, I'll pick you up around six then," Steve Murdoch said.

As we were watching Mr. Murdoch head back to his truck, I saw E.B. drive by. The only vehicles allowed on

Main Street were the ones belonging to folks who were selling stuff. After they unloaded everything, the sellers were supposed to park their trucks and vans in the main parking lot behind Sanborn's Department Store. I waved to E.B. and Nanny Jo, but they didn't see me.

"I'll be back in a minute," I told Ed Earl. "I got to talk to Nanny Jo."

Ed Earl was busy messing around with the calculator he'd brought. It was the kind that printed out the figures on a roll of paper, and he was planning on using it to make receipts for the customers. He also had a small metal box to hold the money and make change.

"I hope these batteries hold out all day," he said. "I forgot to change them this morning."

"You heard a word I said?"

He looked up at me with his blank, pale face. "Of course. You said you were going to talk to Nanny Jo." He pushed a few buttons on the calculator and the roll of white paper inched forward. "So what are you standing here for?"

I shook my head. "Who knows," I said, and headed off down the street.

Nanny Jo and E.B. had set up their table right where the craft fair ended and the flea market began. They seemed real pleased to see me.

"I got five new quilts I made," Nanny Jo explained as she arranged them on the table. "Them's the craft part." She hunkered down and opened another box. "These here

147

quilts are antiques. Been in our family for generations."
She began laying them on the other half of the table.
"This here's the flea-market half," she said.

I knew some of those quilts dated back to Nanny Jo's
own grandmother's time. Nanny Jo's grandmother is my
great-great-great-grandmother. Ever since I could remember, Nanny Jo's been real proud of those quilts.

Sometimes, when she was in the right mood, she would
spread one of them out and tell me the stories behind it.
Like where some of the scraps of material came from. One
quilt was made almost entirely from bits and pieces of old
clothes Nanny Jo and her sisters and brothers wore when
they were kids. I always called it the story quilt.

Even after all these years, Nanny Jo can still point to a
piece of blue-and-white checked calico in that quilt and
tell me how it had been the only dress she had owned
when she was five. And how her mama had made a little
calico doll out of the leftover material. Nanny Jo said that
was a real luxury back then. You didn't waste material on
frivolous things like dolls.

I looked down at those quilts that had been in my family for so many years, that held all that history in those
little strips of cloth, and felt like I'd left my insides back
home. All this time I'd believed Nanny Jo when she said
she was leaving the family quilts to me and my sisters
someday. And she'd always promised me I'd get the story
quilt. Now she was going to sell them off to strangers.

Folks who didn't know anything about the stories that went along with them. Tears started stinging the corners of my eyes.

I could feel Nanny Jo and E.B. watching me. I guess they were expecting me to say something. But before I could, Nanny Jo said, "It's about what's most important, Quinny girl. These old quilts might help save our home and groves. That land's been there as long as any of them quilts." She rested her wrinkled hand on my shoulder. "That's part of your heritage, too. And I ain't about to see it mined under."

"But why the story quilt?" I said. "You got all those other ones you can sell."

E.B. gave my arm a squeeze. "It ain't easy on Nanny Jo, either, sugar."

Suddenly, right in the middle of what E.B. was saying, Nanny Jo got this puzzled look on her face. For a minute I thought she was going to start blinking, like Pa-Daddy does. She took a step back like she was sizing me up for something. "What you doing here anyway, Quinnella? Your daddy know you're here?"

"No ma'am." There's no lying to Nanny Jo. She can always tell. She'll just keep staring you down till that old lie pops right up and announces itself. "Me and Ed Earl made cypress-knee lamps to sell at the craft fair, so we can donate money to help. Rhonda Fay's here, too."

"Oh, your daddy's gonna love this when he hears it,"

Nanny Jo said, but I could tell she was pleased. Then she pinched my cheek. "That's my girl," she said. "Can't keep us Ellerbees down, right?"

E.B. had his nose tilted toward the clouds, sniffing the air. "Mmm-mm," he said. "Something smells mighty good."

"Smells like hush puppies," I said.

"Why don't I go get us some?" he said, heading off toward the food stands.

"Nanny Jo," I said, after E.B. had left, "any mail come for me?"

She handed me two corners of a quilt, then took the other two. "Nothing yet," she said. We shook the quilt a few times, then folded it up and set it on the table. "Maybe your mama didn't leave no forwarding address," Nanny Jo said. "So the post office couldn't send it on to her."

I nodded. "Maybe." But I still wanted to believe my postcard had reached her.

E.B. showed up then with a whole mess of hush puppies, including an extra plate for me to take back to Rhonda Fay and Ed Earl so we could all have something to eat. Ed Earl had packed a lunch of peanut-butter-and-banana sandwiches for the three of us for later, but right then those hush puppies really hit the spot.

I don't know when I'd ever seen so many folks in one place. They were like ants on a sugarcoated anthill. Must have been thousands. Not just from our county, but from all over. I figured the Pines's organizing committee must have done one heck of a job advertising the fair.

I'd brought along a pad and pencil so I could interview people in between selling lamps. After all, this was the biggest event folks had seen in a long time. This was *news*. I figured maybe I could write all about what happened and give the story to the local paper. If it was good enough, maybe they would print it.

Course, Rhonda Fay was practically no help at all. She spent most of the day wandering from table to table socializing. But even without her, we sold six lamps, which Ed Earl said was pretty good considering it was mostly locals who came to the fair. Folks around here don't have much money, and they sure don't have fifty dollars to fritter away on a lamp made out of an old cypress knee. Ed Earl figured there were probably a few tourists mixed in with the crowd, which was why we did so good.

I told him to consider those six lamps part of my seven-lamp inventory, but he said he wanted to make a contribution, too. So we split it. The money we made from three lamps was mine to donate, and the rest was his.

"My dad says there's a big meeting at the high school tonight," Ed Earl told me while he sat there counting our money. "It's for the folks that are for the mining company coming in, and the ones that are against it." He set a handful of ten-dollar bills aside and started on the fives. "The

151

meeting's supposed to help folks understand each other's positions better, so maybe they can find some sort of solution."

I wasn't sure how to take this latest development. What kind of solution? I wondered if Pa-Daddy knew anything about the meeting. But it turned out I didn't have long to wonder. I mean, there we were, all feeling pretty good about the way the fair and flea market had gone, when I suddenly spotted Pa-Daddy's pickup. It was down by the wood barriers that the local sheriff had put up to block off Main Street during the fair. Pa-Daddy was staring right at me. It was like a laser beam was shooting right from his eyes straight into my heart. I could tell he was madder than I'd ever seen him in my entire life.

14

Drawing the Line

Ed Earl was still busy counting the money, for the hundredth time that day. His hair kept brushing his eyelashes the whole time he was leaning over the cash box, but he didn't bother to push it back.

I didn't want Pa-Daddy making a scene in front of Ed Earl. He didn't know a thing about how Pa-Daddy was counting on the new mining company for work, and I wanted to keep it that way.

I wondered where Rhonda Fay had suddenly got to, and if she knew Pa-Daddy was there. Up until a few minutes ago, she'd been helping Ed Earl count money. Then out of the corner of my eye I spotted something near my foot. It looked like the toe of Rhonda Fay's sneaker. I bent down and took a peek under the table. There she was, all hunched up into a little ball.

"Anybody ever tell you you've got the brain of a turnip?" I said.

"Hush up, Quinn." She started smacking my leg with her hand, trying to get me to move on. "Pa-Daddy's truck is over there. I don't want him to see me."

"Rhonda Fay, if you were born with any sense at all, you'd know he can see you clear as if you were standing two feet in front of him. You aren't fooling anybody."

I stood up and walked over to Ed Earl. I was hoping he had been too busy counting money to notice Rhonda Fay making a fool of herself. "I got to go see somebody," I told him, heading off in the direction of Pa-Daddy's truck. "I'll be right back."

Ed Earl nodded without bothering to look up. I bet he didn't even lose count of that handful of five-dollar bills he was holding.

Pa-Daddy saw me coming, but he didn't get out of the pickup. He sat up there, way above me, surveying the fair and all the folks. Without even looking at me, he said, "What you doing here, Quinnella?" He sounded like Nanny Jo.

I knew Pa-Daddy was waiting for my answer, but I was having trouble breathing, and my heart was thumping like an old tom-tom. Me and Pa-Daddy had done our share of feuding lately, but I'd never outright gone against him before. Still, I knew this wasn't the time to back down. I knew I had to give him a straight answer. "Helping," I said, jerking my chin forward so he'd know I meant business.

Pa-Daddy tipped his engineer's hat toward the back of his head. "Helping who?" he said, still without looking at me. His voice was low and flat.

I didn't dare let on how much he scared me right then. Even the roots of my hair felt prickly, like the night the lightning from the storm struck the tree on our road, splitting it right down the middle.

"I'm helping Nanny Jo and E.B. and all my other friends from my old school—all those folks who moved to the Pines from Panther Ridge," I said. "I'm helping them to keep their homes."

"You don't think *I* need your help?" he said, finally turning his face toward me. It was a look I hope I'll never have to see again as long as I live. There was a mountain of pain and anger all froze together on that face. "You don't think having no money for food or a roof over our heads requires a little family support?" His voice was slow and even. Each word fell on my heart like a brick.

"Pa-Daddy," I said, mustering all the courage I could, "I did a lot of thinking on this whole mining situation. And the truth is, I don't believe what you're doing is the best thing."

Pa-Daddy's jaw twitched like he was getting ready to say something, but I didn't give him a chance. I was afraid if he got his say before I was finished, I'd lose my nerve.

155

"I know there's a better way," I said. "There's got to be. You can go to work for Nanny Jo and E.B. You could manage their groves." I could tell right off that didn't set well with him. We'd been over this same territory a hundred times before. Usually he just shut me off like I was some old squeaky bedspring he didn't want to listen to. Even now, I wasn't sure he was listening to me. Nanny Jo says winning someone over to your side is like drops of water on a rock. One drop doesn't do diddly. But keep those drops coming one right after the other, and sooner or later you're gonna wear that rock down. So I kept it up, pouring out those same old arguments, hoping Pa-Daddy would change his mind.

"You could learn to do some other kind of work. You don't have to work just in the phosphate mines," I suggested. "It isn't the only job in the world."

"I'm not here to argue this with you, Quinnella. Get in the truck."

I looked back at our table to see if Ed Earl was watching. Or worse, Tanner or Mary Alice. I didn't want anyone to see me getting humiliated in public. "I can't do that," I said.

"What?"

"I'm not coming with you, Dad," I said.

"Dad? Oh, now it's 'Dad.'"

I hadn't even realized I'd called him that, but it seemed fitting at the moment.

Pa-Daddy's hand hit the door handle and his booted foot crashed against the metal, flinging that door wide open. He was on the ground in a flash. Only a few feet of sandy soil stood between us.

I don't know why I did it, but suddenly I stuck the toe of my sneaker in the soil and drew a line, just like I'd done the day we moved. Pa-Daddy stared down at it. "What's that supposed to mean?" he snarled.

"It means we don't see eye to eye on much anymore."

Pa-Daddy narrowed his eyes at me like he wasn't quite sure who this person was he was talking to. "We don't need to see eye to eye," he said. "I'm your father. And I'm telling you to get in the truck."

It still didn't matter to him what I thought. I could feel my ears getting hot. I was so angry I forgot all about being scared. "I'm never going back to that Swamp House," I said.

He snickered some at that one. "You don't say. Well, then, just where else do you figure to get free room and board?"

"Nanny Jo's," I blurted out without thinking. "I'm going to live with Nanny Jo and E.B."

Pa-Daddy's smirky grin slid right off his face. "You mind telling me what this is all about, Quinnella? You been behaving downright ornery lately. I think it's about time you told me what's going on."

"Why should I? Do you ever bother to tell us what's

going on? Did you ever bother to ask us if we wanted to live in some old mosquito-infested swamp? Did you ever ask us if we'd mind doing without electricity or plumbing? Did you ever ask if we wanted to go to another school? Did you care when Ms. Prickett made Mary Alice editor of the sixth-grade newspaper because I was moving away? And after I'd spent a whole year working on my grammar, and for what? So I could talk proper to the swamp gators? Did you care about Mary Alice and her friends calling me the Swamp Thing?" It was like the brakes holding me back had suddenly given out. There was no stopping me. I was careening down a hill at top speed. My mouth just shifted into automatic pilot.

"Did you ever ask us if we felt bad about Mom leaving? No. You just wouldn't let us talk about her, like she'd never been a part of our lives at all." I threw up my hands. I was yelling loud as could be. But I didn't care if the whole world heard me.

"You just let her go, like she was some old dishrag that blew off the clothesline in a storm. You didn't even think she was worth going after. You just let her go. Just like you're gonna let Nanny Jo's place go. You'd let that new mining company tear down the house and groves without so much as a sneeze in their direction. That's my family history, Pa-Daddy. And Rhonda Fay's and Louise's. It belongs to us. But you don't even care about family anymore. You just let everything go . . . can't mine phosphate, so you won't do nothing else . . . just let the bank have the Swamp House . . . don't do nothing . . . drink beer . . . shoot dead branches . . ." I knew I was just babbling. I wasn't making much sense. Not even to myself.

Pa-Daddy hadn't said a word. He just let me go on like a raving magpie. "A piece of seaweed's got more backbone than you. You think you got no choices. You think you can't do nothing about the stuff that's happened to you," I said, slipping back into my old way of talking. Maybe I thought he'd understand me better that way. "But that ain't true. You can at least try."

I stared down at the line I'd made with my sneaker and shook my head. Things were calming down inside me. I felt like my bones had dissolved and it would only be a few seconds before the rest of me shriveled into a little pile of skin lying in the sand.

"I'm sorry," I said. My voice was getting hoarse from all my shouting. "I just can't stand it anymore, watching you give up so easy all the time."

Pa-Daddy took a step back, like he thought I might hit him. He rocked a little on his heels, unsteady, then climbed back into the truck. Without saying another word, he turned the key, and the engine of the pickup let out a roar. He shifted into reverse, then looked over his shoulder to see if anything was behind him. "I got a meeting to go to," he said, still looking over his shoulder. "See that Nanny Jo gives you a good supper. You can come pick up your belongings tomorrow."

Then he was gone. A cloud of dust followed the pickup down the road. And not once, during all that time, had he ever stepped over my line.

15

The Meeting

First thing Rhonda Fay wanted to know, when I got back to the table, was were we grounded for life.

"He didn't say anything about grounding us," I told her. Then it hit me: Pa-Daddy hadn't even seemed to notice Rhonda Fay was there. He'd never once mentioned her. I wondered what he would do when he found out not one, but two of his daughters were traitors, which was how he was sure to see it. Still, I was proud I'd stuck to my guns.

Ed Earl was packing the leftover lamps in boxes. "My dad's going to be here any minute," he said.

"I'm not riding home with you," I told him.

Rhonda Fay stood there scratching a mosquito bite till it bled. She cocked her head to one side, staring at me. "How you going to get home?" she said.

"With Nanny Jo and E.B." I didn't feel like telling her right then that I wasn't going home at all. That I wasn't ever going to live in the Swamp House again.

"Well, then I'm going with Nanny Jo, too," she said.

"Can't."

"Why not?"

I didn't have an answer for her, so I made one up. "Because Pa-Daddy's mad enough as it is. He said you were to go right home. If you don't do what he says, then he'll ground you for sure."

Rhonda Fay eyed me suspiciously. "Then how come you don't have to go right home?"

"Because I'm going to help Nanny Jo pack up first," I lied.

"Why can't I help?"

"Rhonda Fay," I said, puffing out my cheeks in exasperation, "just do what Pa-Daddy said, okay? We're in enough trouble."

I could tell she still wasn't buying my story, and she would have kept on arguing with me till doomsday. But then Mr. Murdoch pulled up in his pickup, and we had to help him and Ed Earl load up.

I explained to Mr. Murdoch I wasn't going home with him, and he seemed fine with that. The thing was, after they left, it suddenly occurred to me that I'd never even mentioned moving in to Nanny Jo. Course, I was family. She wasn't going to turn me away. But I started feeling a bit unsettled, wondering if maybe I should have asked her first.

E.B. and Nanny Jo were just getting ready to pack up the quilts when I got to their table. There weren't many left. I looked for the story quilt, but it was gone. I told myself I had to be grown-up about it. Folks had to do what they had to do. But what I really wanted was to sit right down on the sidewalk and burst into tears.

Nanny Jo was watching me as she stuffed a quilt into a large box. "E.B. sold it," she said, "while I was off getting a bite of lunch." She sighed, then pulled another quilt from the table. "Better that way," she said. "Not knowing who bought it, I mean."

I nodded. I understood what Nanny Jo meant. If she knew the person who'd bought it, she might be tempted to buy it back. That's what I would've tried to do.

I looked over at E.B. I think maybe he felt bad about selling the quilt. But he'd only done what Nanny Jo had told him to. "You'd better run along, sugar," he told me. "You don't want to miss your ride."

I didn't know what to say to that. Suddenly I felt like I didn't belong anyplace. Not the Swamp House, not Nanny Jo's.

E.B. patted me on the head and helped Nanny Jo into the pickup. "You head on back, now," he said, climbing in the other side.

They were leaving and I hadn't even told them I was

163

going to be living with them. "Wait," I shouted as E.B. revved up the engine. Nanny Jo stuck her head out the window. A light breeze lifted that bird-feather hair of hers into the air. For a minute it looked like her hair might float right off her head. "I missed my ride," I said. Boy, this lying thing was really getting out of control.

They looked over at where my table had been. Sure enough, the Murdochs and Rhonda Fay had disappeared.

"What could those folks have been thinking, taking off without you like that?" Nanny Jo said, moving closer to E.B. to make room for me. "Well, hop on in."

"We got us a little problem, sugar," E.B. said. "Your grandma and me has an important meeting to go to at the high school. We can't take you home right now."

"That's okay," I said, figuring I was buying myself a little more time to decide how to tell them I wasn't going home anyway. "I'll just come to the meeting with you."

E.B. seemed to be studying the situation while we all sat there in the unmoving truck, right in the middle of Main Street. "I don't know, sugar. This meeting ain't no place for younguns. If we take you along, you got to promise to stay in the truck while we're inside. Maybe your daddy will be there. He can give you a ride home after the meeting."

Nanny Jo let out a little snort. "You can bet the farm he'll be there."

Hearing Pa-Daddy's name got those peanut-butter-and-banana sandwiches to doing a little dance in my stomach. I hadn't thought about seeing him there. But he had said he had a meeting to go to. I should have guessed.

Truth is, I was getting pretty excited about this meeting business. It sounded real important. I patted the pocket of my cutoffs. My pad and pencil were still there. If I could get inside the school and find out what was happening, it might make a great news story. Besides, I really wanted to know what was going on. So I promised E.B. I would stay in the truck when we got there, knowing darn well I was planning to do just the opposite.

As soon as E.B. parked the pickup and they went inside, I climbed down and headed straight for the front door of the high school. The halls were empty, but I could tell right off where the meeting was on account of all the noise coming from the auditorium.

I eased one of the doors open and slipped inside, keeping my back against the wall. The room was so packed with folks, I figured nobody would notice me anyway. All the seats were taken, and there wasn't much standing room left. I looked around for Pa-Daddy, but I didn't see him anywhere, the place being so crowded and all. I did spot Nanny Jo and E.B. sitting down front. I was glad they had their backs to me.

Some of the folks in the audience were standing up, booing and hissing at some poor man on the stage. I tugged on the dress sleeve of this old woman I was standing next to. She gave me an annoyed look like I was a puppy trying to undo her shoelaces or something.

"Who's that man on the stage?" I asked her.

"Reed Wallace, the high-school principal," she hissed at me. I could tell she didn't want some kid interrupting her listening.

Reed Wallace was going on about how folks who didn't know anything but mining should take the layoffs as a big chance to start all over again with a whole new career. He said he was going to hand out information on something called the GED, which stands for General Educational Development. He said folks could get a high-school diploma through that program.

That's when Charlie Slater, who used to work with Pa-Daddy at the Panther Ridge Mining Company, stood up and sassed right back at him. "What if we don't want another career, Wallace? How about that? What if we like what we're doing just fine?" A bunch of other folks started applauding old Charlie and shouting stuff at Reed Wallace.

Poor Mr. Wallace stood there on the stage, taking in all those boos and hisses. He was this short, skinny man in a dark-green suit, which in those lights made him look kind of green all over. Finally, after he had patted the air with the palms of his hands a few times, trying to quiet the audience, he pulled the microphone from the podium and shouted for a little order. About time, too. If kids had been behaving that way in the school auditorium, they would have all ended up with a week's detention.

The whole meeting was like that. Whenever somebody got up onstage, whichever side didn't agree with him

166

spent the whole time hissing and booing. So it was hard to even hear what was going on. One guy offered jobs to folks who wanted to learn the tool-and-die-making trade, but he said they had to be good at math, so a lot of people got upset about that.

Then Ed Earl's father got up and talked about the awful things mining was doing to the environment and to people's health. I was really surprised to see him there. I looked around for Ed Earl, but he wasn't anywhere in sight. Neither was Rhonda Fay, so I expect Mr. Murdoch took them home first.

There were some folks in the audience who actually stood up and applauded when he finished talking—probably the Pines folks, figuring this was another good argument they could use. But there was still a lot of booing, and folks yelling about how environmentalist types were always overreacting.

Far as I could tell, nobody was really listening much to what anybody else had to say. When the meeting broke up, folks seemed to be feeling even meaner than when they went in.

I slipped out the door, planning to get back in the truck so Nanny Jo and E.B. would think I had been there the whole time. Besides, I had to write all this stuff down so I wouldn't forget it. But before I even got down the front steps of the school, folks came busting through the door like a herd of penned-up bulls breaking through their fencing. Nobody seemed to be heading for their cars. Instead, they all stood around arguing and shouting at each other.

I saw Pa-Daddy talking to Joe Whiggs. They were looking kind of thoughtful, like they were puzzling over something. Then I saw Charlie Slater come up to them. And a few minutes later, I saw him give Pa-Daddy a shove on his shoulder. But Charlie Slater wasn't the only one shoving, because these folks standing to my left suddenly started taking swipes at each other.

Then all heck broke loose. *Kapow!* Some folks started screaming and running in all directions, and some folks were beating up on each other. I don't know where he came from, but a man I didn't even know was whirling around, swinging a baseball bat in all directions at once. Everybody was pushing and shoving to get out of his way.

I saw E.B. trying to get Nanny Jo off to the side. I headed over to help, just as somebody grabbed my arm and pulled me behind a parked truck.

"Let go," I said, yanking my arm away.

"Quinn, how did you get here? This is no place for kids." I looked up into Steve Murdoch's face.

"My dad's here," I said, as if that explained everything.

Mr. Murdoch stood there pulling at his earlobe like he wasn't sure what to do with me. It made me think of Ed Earl, twisting his hair. "I'm afraid things have gotten out of control," he said. "This is a dangerous place to be right now. I want you to get inside my pickup and stay there." He pulled open the door, grabbed my elbow, and all but lifted me into the front seat. But the minute he left, I climbed down. I was getting tired of folks telling me to stay put inside their trucks.

I went running back to see if I could find Nanny Jo and E.B., and I was just in time to see Andy Eberstadt marching toward the crowd with his hunting rifle. Old Andy isn't wrapped too tight to begin with, and I figured all the feuding was probably getting on his nerves. I cupped my hands around my mouth and yelled at the top of my lungs, "He's got a gun!"

Some folks hit the dirt, facedown. Some stood stockstill, like a rabbit does when it senses danger. They didn't move a muscle. But some folks kept right on beating each other up. One of those folks was Charlie Slater, who was blasting his fists into Pa-Daddy's face as hard and fast as he could.

Everything happened so fast after that, I can't remember but a few bits and pieces, like something had gone and shattered the pictures in my mind. First there was a shot. Then Joe Whiggs went down on his knees, his mouth hanging open like some big gaping hole of surprise. Nanny Jo and E.B. moved toward Pa-Daddy in a kind of jerky slow run, stopping, starting, stopping, then starting again.

Fists first, I pushed and punched my way through the crowd that was gathering around Joe Whiggs. But what I saw when I got there was my dad, lying in a heap on the school walk, and Charlie Slater staring down at him, like

169

he couldn't figure out what had gone wrong. The back of Pa-Daddy's head was on the concrete step, soaked with blood. Joe Whiggs was lying on his side, moaning and holding his right leg. I could tell it was bleeding bad, like Pa-Daddy's head.

I felt like I'd been standing there for hours. But it was more like a few seconds on account of I'd no sooner broke through the crowd than E.B. grabbed my arm and pulled me back.

"Listen to me," he said. "Your daddy's going to be okay. That Mr. Murdoch feller just went inside to call an ambulance." But E.B.'s voice was none too reassuring. He sounded like he had a wad of bubble gum stuck in his throat.

I couldn't do anything but stare back at him. No words were coming out of my mouth. Something in my brain kept telling me none of this was really happening, so not to pay it any mind.

E.B. snatched me by the shoulders and gave me a good long shake. "Did you hear me?"

"Who did Andy shoot?" I asked. My mouth was dry as cotton.

"He shot Joe Whiggs in the knee."

"Was Pa-Daddy shot, too?"

"No. He fell back and hit his head when Charlie laid one on him."

My legs felt like two rubber bands. I wasn't sure they were going to hold me up. I began to shake all over and tears just gushed out of my eyes like a spring flood. There was no stopping them. E.B. pulled a handkerchief from his back pocket, handed it to me, then steered me toward his pickup. Nanny Jo was already inside. Her face was the color of dirty bread dough.

E.B. was helping me into the front seat when we heard the sirens. There were at least four ambulances, coming from all over, lights flashing everywhere. I guess other folks had called, too. Word of the fight must have spread pretty fast.

Nanny Jo didn't say a thing. She just put her bony arm around my shoulders and held me close.

"Stay put," E.B. told me. "I want to find out which hospital they're taking your daddy to."

And for the first time that night, I did what I was told. I didn't so much as stick my big toe outside that truck.

16

The Hospital

I don't remember a night ever being so dark. Not a star in the sky. I couldn't even see the moon. Maybe it was planning to storm. I don't know. I kept thinking how weird it was, after it being such a bright sunny day, to look up and not see any stars.

But the darkness was fitting, somehow, because I felt like some huge darkness was swallowing me up inside. E.B. didn't say much after coming back from the ambulance—only that Pa-Daddy was beat up pretty bad. All I know is that it seemed like whole days had gone by before E.B. finally got back to the truck.

I couldn't get Pa-Daddy off my mind. I kept seeing that scene between us over and over again, and hearing him say, "You don't think *I* need your help?" What if he died before we got to the hospital? I'd never have the chance to

172

set things straight with him, or tell him that even though we didn't see eye to eye on some things, I still loved him.

It seemed like hours before we finally arrived at the hospital, but it probably didn't take us more than ten minutes. E.B. parked near the emergency-room entrance, and we headed inside.

I wasn't crying anymore. Instead, I sat in the waiting area with Nanny Jo, pretending to read some magazine while E.B. went to find out what he could about Pa-Daddy. The glare of the fluorescent lights on the white walls was hurting my eyes, so I closed the magazine and just left it lying there on my lap. Besides, I couldn't much concentrate anyway.

"This feller, Dr. Tyler, is patching him up right now," E.B. told us, wandering back to the sitting area. "The lady at the desk says she'll let the doc know we're here. As soon as he's finished, he'll come out and tell us what's going on."

I nodded and handed him the copy of *Good Housekeeping* that was on my lap, because I didn't know what else to do. But instead of sitting down to read, he laid the magazine back on the table.

"I'm going to ride out to your house and get Louise and Rhonda Fay," he said. "Y'all are staying at our place tonight." Nanny Jo just reached over and patted my hand.

E.B. headed outside. The doors slid closed as I ran after him, then they opened again.

"I need to know how bad it is," I said, coming up behind him. "I can't stand not knowing."

E.B. turned around, then put his arm around my shoulders and gave me a little squeeze. "It's pretty serious, Quinn. I ain't gonna lie to you."

My whole body began to shake and my breathing started to come in bumpy little gulps. Tears were stinging the corners of my eyes again.

"I'm going back inside in case the doctor comes out," I told him, trying to keep my voice normal-sounding.

E.B. nodded, studying me real serious for a minute. I guess he could see how shaky I was. "Want me to come back inside with you for a while longer?"

I thought about that. It was pretty obvious E.B. wanted to get as far from the hospital as he could. The whole family knew he had this terror of hospitals. They really scare the britches off him. It was a wonder he'd stayed as long as he had. "No, I'll be okay," I lied.

It wasn't until an hour later that Dr. Tyler finally came out and asked for Nanny Jo and me. He said he was having Pa-Daddy admitted to the hospital because they wanted to keep him under observation for a few days. Seemed he had a broken nose and something called a depressed fracture of the skull, which meant X rays and tests to find out how serious it was. The doctor was also pretty worried about internal bleeding, because Pa-Daddy had taken a couple of bad punches in the stomach and chest.

This person the doctor called an orderly was going to

wheel my dad up to a place called the Intensive Care Unit. The doctor told us we could go on up to see Pa-Daddy, but we could stay only ten minutes. He said there wasn't much we could say or do, seeing as how Pa-Daddy was still unconscious.

Dr. Tyler had already warned us that Pa-Daddy had been bruised up pretty bad, but nothing could have prepared me for what I saw when I walked into his room. That man lying in the hospital bed didn't even look like my dad. His eyes were almost swollen shut, his face was covered with cuts and bruises, there was tape across his nose, and his lip had a large purple gash along the bottom. It was swollen, too. Even his knuckles were swollen. And there were all these tubes and things stuck in him.

I couldn't help thinking this was all my fault. If I hadn't wanted out of the Swamp House so bad . . . if I hadn't cooked up that whole dumb plan so we could all go live with Nanny Jo . . . if I hadn't tried to help the Pines folks . . . if I'd at least tried to understand Pa-Daddy's side of it. I mean, he really had been trying to find work, digging ditches and all. If only I'd listened to Louise . . . if, if, if. But all those *if*s didn't mean a thing now, because it was too late.

Nanny Jo gave my hand a squeeze, like she was trying to pass along some of her courage.

"Pa-Daddy," I whispered, moving closer to the bed. For a second I thought I saw his head shift a little, but I was probably only kidding myself. I sat by the bed and stroked his arm awhile. There didn't seem to be much else to do, him being unconscious and all.

A few minutes later E.B. showed up with Louise and Rhonda Fay. Rhonda Fay was sobbing and sniffling and wiping her eyes and nose on her soggy T-shirt. Louise wasn't crying, but her face was red and puffy. Neither of them said anything to me.

Nanny Jo took them both up to see Pa-Daddy while me and E.B. went outside for some fresh air. We walked around the hospital parking lot for a while, then E.B. put his hand on my shoulder. We both stopped walking. "Quinn honey," he said, "your daddy's gonna be all right. I don't want you thinking otherwise."

If I could have took off running without him catching me, I would have done it. I had a powerful need to be leaving all this behind. I don't know why, but suddenly I thought of Comfort Creek. I found myself wishing it was a real place, because if it was, I knew that's just where I'd run to.

"How would you know?" I blurted out. "Even that doctor doesn't know if he'll be okay."

The parking-lot light overhead spread our shadows over the pavement like a couple of oil slicks. I started walking away from E.B. I didn't have the faintest notion where I was headed, but it seemed important to keep moving right then.

"You got to hold on, Quinn," E.B. said, catching up to

me. "I know this has been a real tough time for you. And with your ma not here—"

"Shut up! I don't have to listen to you," I said, covering my ears. "I don't want to hear any more." With my hands over my ears, my voice sounded like it was coming from inside a tunnel. "My life's been nothing but losing things lately. There isn't any more room. I'm all filled up with losing things. If you keep talking, I'm going to explode. You hear? *Explode!*" I threw my arms out like I was about to do just that.

E.B. reached out and grabbed my arm. But I pushed his hand away and gave him a good swift kick in the shin. He flinched, but he didn't say anything.

"I am a very angry person right now," I screamed, warning him too late.

I couldn't believe I had kicked poor old E.B. The minute I did it, I felt bad. But it was worse than that, because what I really wanted to do was hit him again. I wanted to run at him with my fists and punch him as hard as I could. I wanted to scream at him, kick him, punch his lights out if I had to.

But I knew it wasn't E.B. I was mad at. Anybody could have been standing there in front of me, even the President of the United States himself. I would have kicked him in the shin, too. It didn't matter who it was. All that mattered was the punching and the kicking.

Then, for one tiny moment, I thought I understood

why all those folks had gotten themselves into such a ruckus earlier. Sure there wasn't any sense to it. But I guess all those smashed hopes, all those lost jobs filled them up till there wasn't any more room. They were like sticks of dynamite stuffed full of gunpowder, just waiting. It was true Pa-Daddy had messed up my career plans, but for him it had been even worse. He'd lost the only job he'd ever had. I knew I'd been feeling pretty resentful about what he'd done to me. But I figured he must have been feeling even madder at what the company had done to him. Mad as blazes. Not that the fighting made it right. What all those folks did was wrong, pure and simple. But at least, now, I could sort of understand it. If my life had been full of losing things, so had Pa-Daddy's. That's what Louise had been trying to tell me.

Shaking all over, I stared up at E.B. Then I spun around and gave the metal pole of the parking-lot light a good whack with my fist.

"Did it help?" E.B. said quietly.

I stared down at my hand. Two of the knuckles had started bleeding. "It hurts like hell," I said.

He reached in his back pocket for his handkerchief, but it wasn't there. I guess he forgot he had given it to me earlier. So he wrapped his own hand around mine like he was making a bandage. "I know," he said. And we both knew I wasn't talking about my hand.

We started walking back to the hospital. "You got one mean weapon there," E.B. said, pointing to my foot, the one I had kicked him with. "I'm gonna start calling you the Karate Kid."

I knew he was trying to make me laugh, but I couldn't. I sure did appreciate him trying, though.

17

Pa-Daddy

Well, as it turned out, we all had a big surprise waiting for us when we got to the hospital the next afternoon. Dr. Tyler told us the little piece of bone in Pa-Daddy's head wasn't pressing against his brain or causing something called internal hemorrhaging, so they weren't going to have to operate. He said there didn't seem to be any brain damage, which we were all real relieved about.

The best part was that Pa-Daddy was wide awake and looking a little more like himself. The swelling had gone down some, but the bruises were still there. So was the nasty split on his lip.

He wasn't in the Intensive Care Unit anymore. They had moved him to a double room, but there wasn't anybody in the other bed. His lunch tray still sat on the table beside him. He hadn't eaten much. I couldn't blame him.

It was all soft, mushy-looking stuff, I guess on account of his mouth being sore and all. He tried to smile when he saw us, but I could tell it hurt, because he winced a little.

There were only two chairs, so I sat myself next to Pa-Daddy on the bed—real careful, though. Rhonda Fay stood at the foot of the bed like she was afraid to come any closer. Louise just hovered in the doorway, then wandered over and sat on the other bed, while E.B. and Nanny Jo helped themselves to the two chairs.

"Doc says all the X rays are fine. No broken bones, no cracked ribs, just a busted nose," Pa-Daddy said, reaching over and patting my hand. It was like he'd forgot all about our fight at the fair the day before. But I didn't want to fool myself into thinking things were going to be the way they had been before all this happened. Still it felt good to know Pa-Daddy was happy to see me, because I sure was glad to see him.

"Doc Tyler says they won't have to operate," Nanny Jo said.

"Guess it wasn't as bad as they thought," Pa-Daddy told us. "That's what comes of being so hardheaded." He laughed, but nobody else did. "I should be out of this place in a few days."

"Probably got your head messed up when Charlie Slater gave you that right to the jaw," E.B. said. "You went over like a felled tree. That old head of yours landed right on them front steps."

"Yeah?" Pa-Daddy looked like he was trying to remember what had happened. "About the last thing I seen was old Charlie's fist coming straight at me."

Suddenly it dawned on me. Something about the fight didn't make any sense. Why would Charlie Slater, who was one of Pa-Daddy's working buddies from the Panther Ridge mine, take a swipe at my dad? Charlie Slater was on Pa-Daddy's side, wasn't he?

"How come Charlie hit you?" I asked him. "He's supposed to be on your side."

"Were you taking sides with the Pines folks?" Rhonda Fay said, leaving her post at the foot of the bed and hopping up next to Louise.

"Now don't go jumping to conclusions." Pa-Daddy snorted through his broken nose. "I'll tell you, though, by the time that meeting let out, a lot of folks had started doing some serious thinking. Joe Whiggs was even going on about maybe studying for some of those GED tests. We got to talking about it outside, after the meeting. I guess Charlie Slater didn't much like what he was hearing. Figured we'd sold him out, gone over to the other side. He and a few of his buddies decided they was going to help change our minds right back to where they was before."

E.B. and I exchanged glances. I knew he was wondering, like me, if Pa-Daddy knew Joe Whiggs had been shot in the leg. Pa-Daddy was watching us. "I been down to see Joe," he said, like he'd read our minds. "He's doing just fine. Why don't you folks stop in and say howdy before you leave. He'd like that. He's right down the hall there."

I took Pa-Daddy's big hand and rubbed it against my cheek. The calluses on his palm felt rough against my skin.

Then he said, right out of the blue, "How about everybody going down to the cafeteria for some ice cream while I talk to Quinn, here." He looked over at me with his swollen eyes. "We got a few things we need to get off our chests."

My heart about slipped into my stomach when he said that. I just knew he was going to bring up what I'd said to him after the craft fair. I wanted to grab everybody and tell them not to leave me alone with him, but they were already out the door.

But Pa-Daddy just reached over and rubbed his big swollen hand along my shoulder, giving it a squeeze. "Yesterday, when you brought up your mom . . . well, I figured out what you'd really been mad about all this time. Why maybe you been behaving so ornery lately." He took a deep breath, and I could tell it hurt him because of the bruises on his chest and all. "I'm real sorry about what happened with your mom," he said, his voice thick as syrup. "After I got that letter saying she wanted a divorce, I just couldn't stand hearing folks talk about her no more. But it wasn't right, telling you kids not to ever mention her name again. I can see that now."

He gave a strand of my hair a little tug. "I knew she

wasn't the marrying kind the day I met her, but I just had to have her anyway," he said. "I was just a nineteen-year-old kid, crazy in love."

"Then why didn't you make her stay with us?" I said.

"Love don't work that way, darlin'. Your mom would have ended up resenting the heck out of me if I'd kept her from doing what she loved best: being on the road, performing for folks. It wasn't like I didn't want to go after her. I just knew it wasn't what *she* wanted."

"I miss her," I said, hoping I wouldn't make Pa-Daddy angry all over again.

He closed his eyes and swallowed hard. "Me too, Quinn. I miss her something fierce. Sometimes the pain's so bad I don't want to get out of bed in the morning because it would mean facing another day without her."

I knew just how he felt. And Pa-Daddy was right: I had been upset over not being allowed to talk about Mom. And mad because he hadn't gone after her. The truth is, though, I'd also been mad as blazes at *Mom*. But she wasn't there to holler at, and Pa-Daddy was. Not that he didn't get me all riled up, too, especially with all that moving business. But what my mom did was wrong, to my way of thinking—leaving her family like that, hurting Pa-Daddy that way. Still, like Pa-Daddy said, I guess you had to let folks do what they needed to do. We couldn't make her love us by keeping her from her dreams.

"There's something else," he said. "I done something I'm not real proud of." He pointed to the drawer of the table next to his bed and told me to hand him his wallet. He fumbled around with it a bit, on account of his swollen knuckles, and then he pulled out a piece of cardboard with this little key taped to it.

"You take this," he said. "Tell E.B. to drive you back over to the house. In my closet there's a metal box."

"What's in it?" I asked him.

"The deed to the house, insurance policies, stuff like that."

"Why you telling me to get those?" I was starting to get scared. What if he was sicker than we all thought? What if the doctors weren't telling us the truth? I guess Pa-Daddy could see I was getting worried. He waved his big hand at me.

"That's not all that's in there," he said. "There's some letters. Letters your mom's been writing to us. The post office has been forwarding them from our old address."

The first thing that popped into my head was, How could he do this to us? How could he keep us from reading Mom's letters? There I was, getting mad at him all over again, and wishing he'd stop saying stuff I didn't want to hear.

"I told you I wasn't proud of what I did," Pa-Daddy said. "The thing is, I guess, maybe I wanted to shut her out of our lives, like she done to us. I know that's no excuse. I was wrong to keep those letters from you. And I'm real sorry about that." He let out this heavy sigh. "I don't expect you to understand, but sometimes I'm not sure who I am anymore. Things used to be so clear, back when your mom was with me, when I had my job."

Well, Pa-Daddy was right. I didn't understand. I mean, how could a person not know who he was? Maybe I'd figure it all out someday, when I was a grown-up, but for now, all I could think to say was, "You're my dad. That's who you are."

I leaned over and kissed him on the cheek. Real gentle, trying to avoid the bruised spots. Which *didn't* mean I was finished being mad at him. It's just that he looked so down, I wanted to say something to cheer him up. "It's okay, Pa-Daddy, maybe you don't have Mom or a job, but you got all of us, the family." He just smiled at that, and didn't say anything. He knew, like I did, that we'd always be there to see each other through the hard times.

18

Comfort Creek

About a week after Pa-Daddy got out of the hospital, he
called a family meeting. He even invited Nanny Jo and
E.B. We all sat around the kitchen table drinking iced tea
and eating chocolate cake that Nanny Jo had brought with
her.

"I'll tell you, folks," Pa-Daddy said, "lying there in that
hospital bed, with nothing much else to do but think, you
get to putting things in order, deciding what's really important. And I can't think of anything more important
than this family all sticking together, all of us." He looked
over at Nanny Jo, who nodded her approval.

"So I been thinking." Pa-Daddy shifted his eyes toward
E.B. and winked. "How would y'all like to live at Nanny
Jo's? At least till I can get some things straightened out."

Boy, this was downright amazing! Nanny Jo was right.

That old drops-of-water-on-a-rock thing really did work. Pa-Daddy was living proof. Seemed like he'd heard some of what I'd been saying, after all.

"Live at Nanny Jo's?" Rhonda Fay said, like she couldn't quite believe her ears. "With electricity? With a bathroom? With a phone? Like normal folks?"

"Yup." Pa-Daddy gave her cheek a little pinch. "For a while, anyway."

Well, you'd have thought we'd won the lottery, there was so much excitement. Everybody started talking at once, but the general feeling was that we were all in favor of it.

But Pa-Daddy said we had to vote on it, anyway. He said that's how things were going to be around here from now on. Everybody would get their say before he made any big family decisions.

"But what about our house?" Louise said, looking worried. "Is the bank going to take it?"

"No," Pa-Daddy said. "E.B. and I have worked that out. I'm going to take over Nanny Jo's groves for him."

"So I can enjoy a little retirement time," E.B. chimed in. Then he licked the chocolate frosting off his fork.

I wondered when Pa-Daddy and E.B. had made these new arrangements. But I knew Pa-Daddy'd already been over to Nanny Jo's twice that week, so I figured they must have worked it all out then. I could tell Nanny Jo was real pleased. She started cutting everybody a second piece of cake before they'd even asked.

"With the money I make from managing the groves, I'll be able to keep up the payments on the house while we're staying at Nanny Jo's," Pa-Daddy said, plunging his fork into his cake. "One of these days we'll have real plumbing and electricity." Which meant, of course, the house was still staying in the swamp, and someday we'd be moving back there. So even if we were staying at Nanny Jo's for a while, it wouldn't be forever. Still, things were looking pretty good at the moment.

I figured Pa-Daddy had probably been feeling bad about what I'd said the night of the craft fair . . . about him just springing nasty surprises on us and never asking how we felt about anything. I guess he decided he'd make it up to us by moving us all to Nanny Jo's. It was the only way he could be sure we'd have electricity and plumbing and three decent meals a day.

Later on, when me and Pa-Daddy were sitting out on the front porch by ourselves, finishing up the last of the iced tea, I asked him how he was going to manage living at Nanny Jo's with her trying to run his life all the time. I'd been worrying about that ever since I found out we'd be staying there. I knew how he felt about it.

But he just leaned back in the rocker and put his feet up on the porch rail, like he wasn't all that bothered. "Well, I'll just have to stand up to her, won't I," he said. "She can't run my life if I don't let her."

I had to agree with him on that.

"Who knows," Pa-Daddy said, his voice getting kind of

dreamy. "Maybe I'll save up enough money and move us all to Comfort Creek someday."

I knew he was just teasing me. "There's no such place," I reminded him. "Nanny Jo made it up."

"You sound pretty sure about that," he said. "But you know, when I was in the hospital, I got to thinking about those old stories. And sometimes it seemed like I really remember that place. Like I really knew it. And all them people, too. All those folks Nanny Jo told stories about." He put his hands behind his head and leaned back, like he was doing some serious thinking.

"Pa-Daddy," I said, real careful. "Maybe it was that funny medicine they were giving you in the hospital that made you think it was real."

He just laughed at that. "What I mean is, those folks she made up, they sort of remind me of people I know."

"Like who?" I asked him.

"Well, like those Judd and Clem stories she used to tell me and Jeb when we was kids. They were these two brothers who were always picking on each other, sort of like me and Jeb. Only in Nanny Jo's stories, it was always funny, the stuff they used to pull on each other."

I thought about the Nell stories Nanny Jo used to tell. I guess, in a way, Nell was a lot like me. "You might be on to something, Pa-Daddy," I said.

He nodded. And the two of us sat back to dream on the stars for a while.

A few days later we packed up our clothes and headed over to Nanny Jo's, which was about as good as things could get, as far as I was concerned. Except for missing Ed Earl, of course. Part of me is hoping Pa-Daddy'll take to loving the groves the way Nanny Jo does, so we'll get to stay there permanent. But I don't want to get my hopes up too high. At least Pa-Daddy can make the mortgage payments now. And each week he puts any leftover money into what he calls the electricity fund.

It sure is good to be back at school with all my old friends, even if Mary Alice Taylor still got to be the editor of our sixth-grade newspaper. I don't care, because Jim Albritton, who's the editor at *The Mayville Chronicle,* really liked my story about the craft fair and all the stuff that happened. Especially the part about Pa-Daddy and Joe Whiggs and Charlie Slater. He called it a great human-interest story and said he'd publish it. So old Mary Alice can be the sixth-grade editor. Who cares? *My* story's going to be published in a real newspaper.

Meantime the Pines folks have hired this big-time city lawyer from Miami. Nanny Jo says he's doing a fine job of tying everything up in knots, so that mining company isn't going to be moving in anytime soon. She says she expects there's going to be a lot of hollering on both sides before this thing is settled. But at least we've bought ourselves a little time.

The other thing is, I talked old Louise into stopping by the guidance counselor's office at her school and picking up information on the GED. Louise says I'm just wasting my time—and hers into the bargain. She could be right about that, but I'm not ready to give up yet. I mean, maybe Pa-Daddy'll decide to go on managing the groves for the rest of his life, which is fine with me. But if he doesn't, then what? There's no mining work. At least not for now. How's he going to get a job without a high-school diploma? The thing is, I get to worrying about these things. Somebody's got to. Which means I still grind my teeth sometimes, but not nearly as much as I used to.

So anyway, I tucked the pamphlet under the pile of Pa-Daddy's mail on the dining-room table. Just one more drop of water on that old rock, right? He never said anything about it. Not that I really expected him to. But a few days later, when I was helping Nanny Jo dust all the rooms, there was the pamphlet, right on the nightstand next to Pa-Daddy's bed. He hadn't thrown it away, which to my way of thinking was a good sign.

Last Sunday, some of the family came over to Nanny Jo's for dinner like they always do. Me and Rhonda Fay and Louise were sitting at one of the picnic tables reading some of Mom's letters. We do that a lot these days. She'd written dozens of letters, some to me, some to my sisters, some to Pa-Daddy, and some to the whole family. We've gobbled up every word, and we're always hungry for more. I figure she didn't get my postcard. But that's okay, because now I have her new address in Biloxi, Mississippi. I've already written her the longest letter of my life, telling her about everything that's been happening to us.

So there we were, reading letters and waiting for somebody to bring out the food, when here came Pa-Daddy, walking across the yard with a big brown plastic trash bag in his arms. And he was grinning like a bear drowning in moonshine.

He came right up to me, and stood there holding that trash bag like it was a mink coat or something. "Got a little surprise for you," he said, lowering the bag into my lap.

Well, I just didn't know what to think about that.

"Open it," Rhonda Fay said, punching me in the arm and grabbing the end of the trash bag in a huff.

So I did. And there, lying in my lap like the crown jewels of England, but worth a whole lot more, was the story quilt. I looked up at Pa-Daddy, but no words would come out. They were all stuck someplace inside me, pressing against my chest.

"Your daddy gave me the money, back before the day of the craft fair," E.B. told me. "He said I was to buy the story quilt for you."

"Did you know?" I asked Nanny Jo.

She shook her head. "Quinny girl, these two menfolks don't tell me nothing about what's going on around here anymore. They got more secrets than the government." But she didn't seem all that upset about it. I think she was just happy Pa-Daddy'd decided to take over the groves for her and E.B.

Then Pa-Daddy told Louise and Rhonda Fay they could each pick out one of Nanny Jo's quilts for themselves and he'd make another donation to the Pines's fund. Louise seemed pretty happy with that. But Rhonda Fay said she'd rather have a new pair of jeans. Pa-Daddy just laughed and said that was fine with him.

Anyway, there I sat with the story quilt in my lap, and Mom's letters spread out all around me, and with my whole family standing around grinning like a bunch of fools (except for Rhonda Fay, who managed to look totally bored). And then I knew that Nanny Jo had been telling us the truth all along. Because suddenly there I was, sitting right smack in the heart of a place called Comfort Creek.

Author's Note

Company towns, like the fictional Panther Ridge, have long been a part of America's industrial history. The Florida phosphate-mining companies, like the coal-mining companies of West Virginia and Pennsylvania, built towns for the miners and their families, offering them affordable housing, access to company stores, and medical care. By the late 1960s, most of the Florida company towns had closed down. Brewster, Florida, was the last of these towns to shut down, and it has since been completely mined under.

Like the Ellerbees, a family sometimes had a choice of buying its home and moving it or finding someplace else to live. Because I wanted to set my story in the present rather than in the 1960s, I have taken a fiction-writer's liberty with this piece of factual information, hoping to give young readers a sense of how much the fate of the phosphate-mining companies could affect their workers. For even after the company towns closed down, mining families continued to live in close-knit communities, their lives very much influenced by, and connected to, whatever happened to the company. Today many of those mines are closing down or have gone bankrupt, leaving those who have known only mining, whose fathers and grandfathers knew only mining, to make new lives for themselves.

About the Author

Joyce McDonald received bachelor's and master's degrees in English from the University of Iowa. After working in publishing for fourteen years, she returned to the academic life, earned a Ph.D. in English from Drew University, and has been teaching at both Drew and East Stroudsburg University for several years. The author of two previous children's books, she lives in New Jersey with her husband, Dwaine, and their five cats.